# MADRIGALI AND CANZONI
# FOR FOUR AND FIVE VOICES

# RECENT RESEARCHES IN THE MUSIC OF THE RENAISSANCE

*James Haar, general editor*

A-R Editions, Inc., publishes seven series of musicological editions
that present music brought to light in the course of current research:

*Recent Researches in the Music of the Middle Ages and Early Renaissance*
Charles M. Atkinson, general editor

*Recent Researches in the Music of the Renaissance*
James Haar, general editor

*Recent Researches in the Music of the Baroque Era*
Christoph Wolff, general editor

*Recent Researches in the Music of the Classical Era*
Eugene K. Wolf, general editor

*Recent Researches in the Music of the Nineteenth and Early Twentieth Centuries*
Rufus Hallmark and D. Kern Holoman, general editors

*Recent Researches in American Music*
H. Wiley Hitchcock, general editor

*Recent Researches in the Oral Traditions of Music*
Philip V. Bohlman, general editor

Each *Recent Researches* edition is devoted to works
by a single composer or to a single genre of composition.
The contents are chosen for their potential interest to scholars
and performers, then prepared for publication according to the
standards that govern the making of all reliable historical editions.

Subscribers to any of these series, as well as patrons of subscribing institutions,
are invited to apply for information about the "Copyright-Sharing Policy"
of A-R Editions, Inc., under which policy any part of an edition
may be reproduced free of charge for study or performance.

Address correspondence to

A-R EDITIONS, INC.
801 Deming Way
Madison, Wisconsin 53717

RECENT RESEARCHES IN THE MUSIC OF THE RENAISSANCE • VOLUMES 84–85

Gioseppe Caimo

# MADRIGALI AND CANZONI FOR FOUR AND FIVE VOICES

Edited by Leta E. Miller

A-R Editions, Inc.

Madison

*Library of Congress Cataloging-in-Publication Data*

Caimo, Gioseppe, d. 1584.
  [Vocal music. Selections]
  Madrigali and canzoni for four and five
voices.

  (Recent researches in the music of the
Renaissance, ISSN 0486-123X ; v. 84–85)
  Italian words; prefatory matter in English.
  Texts with English translations on p.
Edited from eds. published in Milan and
Venice, 1564–1586.
  Includes bibliographical references.
  Contents: Book 1, Madrigali a 4
(1564)—  —Book 4, Madrigali a 5
(1584/85)—From Fiamma ardente : a 5 (1586).

  1. Madrigals (Music), Italian.
2. Part-songs, Italian. I. Miller, Leta E.
II. Title. III. Series.
M2.R2384 vol. 84–85 [M1579]    90-753019
ISBN 0-89579-246-X

# Contents

## Book 4, Madrigali a 5 (1584/85)

### From Fiamma ardente a 5 (1586)

# Preface

In 1943 Alfred Einstein wrote of Gioseppe Caimo, "Like a good playwright who knows how to do justice both to tragedy and comedy, he is a master of both pathos and humor, and it is surprising that so little attention has been paid to him."[1] Einstein's statement might well have been written in 1989. Caimo remains an inconspicuous figure, relegated to a few sentences in most studies of the Italian madrigal. The compositions in the present volume show such obscurity to be undeserved, for they reveal a composer who was not only an able craftsman but in fact a creative master with a genius for rhetoric and drama. Caimo's madrigals span the gamut from simple declamatory works to ones of complex chromaticism. Yet even his lighter pieces, which capture the liveliness of popular song, display the art of the more elevated style.

## Gioseppe Caimo

Little is known of Caimo's life. While records show that for the greater part of his career he was employed as an organist in Milan (first at S. Ambrogio and later at the duomo), other events in his life are poorly documented. Based on the fact that his first publication appeared in 1564, most sources suggest that he was born around 1540. As late as 1574 he was still called a "young man" by an agent for the Bavarian court,[2] even though he already had four sons, two of whom he was willing to leave in Milan to take a job in Bavaria.[3]

Caimo apparently died quite suddenly late in 1584; an announcement of his "bitter and unexpected death" appears in the preface to his second book of *canzonette*, dated 31 October of that year.[4] At the time of his death, his fourth book of madrigals had undoubtedly already gone to press; its preface, dated 20 November 1584 was written by the composer.[5] That Caimo's demise was not anticipated is confirmed by a letter from Cardinal Carlo Borromeo on 6 September 1584, in which he rejected a proposal to hire Paolo Bellasio as organist for the cathedral, saying, "I have here an organist—a man of high quality in this profession and in his customs."[6] This "man of high quality" is most certainly Caimo; it is obvious that Borromeo had no suspicion that the Milan duomo would soon need a new organist.[7]

Caimo was appointed organist at S. Ambrogio by 1564, when a reference to this position appears on the title page of his *Madrigali a 4*.[8] He was apparently already well respected as a composer, for the 1564 madrigal book contains a work written in honor of Maximilian II's sons, who had recently visited Milan.[9]

The composer is cited in a series of letters written between 1570 and 1575 by Gasparo or Prospero Visconti to William V of Bavaria or his brother Ferdinand.[10] The two Viscontis were Milanese agents who actively recruited musicians for the Bavarian court. From their letters we learn that Caimo was high on their list of prospective employees. Prospero Visconti repeatedly urged Duke William to hire Caimo, extolling his abilities at "improvising counterpoint on the organ with rare and beautiful inventiveness."[11] By 1575 prospects of Caimo's moving to Bavaria were quite serious, and the composer was scheduled to appear before Ferdinand, for whom he would improvise a *"fuga,* which your lordship will give him, and in addition [would perform it] many times in inversion and double counterpoint with all of the parts."[12] Visconti promised that an audition would reveal the composer as "a rare virtuoso with a very powerful and rapid technique."[13] However, there is no further mention of this matter in the Visconti correspondence, and it appears that Caimo never accepted a position at the court. The Visconti letters also inform us that Caimo was paid a commission by Duke William as early as 1570,[14] that several of his compositions were sent to Bavaria,[15] that Caimo's uncle was a doctor to the empress,[16] and that the composer was closely associated with Nicola Vicentino.[17] In fact, Vicentino, who had close connections to Milan in his last years,[18] may well have influenced the development of Caimo's style.

The composer's appointment as organist at the Milan duomo occurred before 5 May 1580, on which date he received a salary increase.[19] A second raise in pay, granted on 17 October of the same year, elevated his salary to the level of the *maestro di capella*,[20] indicating that he was obviously "an exceptionally gifted organist with a wide reputation."[21]

## Compositions and Sources

Caimo's extant compositions include two volumes of madrigals (book 1 *a* 4, 1564; and book 4 *a* 5, 1584–85),[22] one volume of canzonette (book 2 *a* 4, 1584), fourteen "madrigali et canzoni" *a* 5 in the collection *Fiamma ardente* (published posthumously in 1586),[23] and the canto part of a volume of three-voiced *Canzoni napolitane* (1566). The present edition includes transcriptions of both madrigal books, as well as the pieces from *Fiamma ardente,* which, though called *napolitane canzoni* in the preface to the collection, in fact display traits of both the madrigal and the canzonetta. The canzonette of 1584 have not been included in this edition both because of space limitations and because they differ substantially in form from the madrigals and the *Fiamma ardente* works.

The *Madrigali a 4* were published by Francesco Moscheni in Milan and dedicated to Count Ludovico Galerato.

IL PRIMO LIBRO DE
MADRIGALI A QUATTRO VOCI
DI GIOSEPPE CAIMO MILANESE,
organista in Santo Ambroggio maggiore di Milano.
Nuovamente da lui fatti, corretti, & dati in luce.
IN MILANO.
Appresso Francesco Moscheni.
1564

In his preface to the work, the composer humbles himself in the typical manner, while praising his patron:

> Wishing to publish these madrigals of mine, truly immature fruits of my badly cultivated garden, I have summoned the boldness to attach them to the honored image of your greatness, not at all in recompense of any part of the infinite obligations that for many virtuous reasons I owe to you, but so that, lit by the brightness of your honored name, they may attract much more favor. May it thus please you, my illustrious lord, to accept them with your usual kindness, with which you bind firmly to yourself the hearts of all.[24]

One copy of this collection survives in the British Library.

The *Madrigali a 5* were issued in Venice by Giacomo Vincenzi and Ricciardo Amadino[25] and dedicated to Antonio Perez, secretary of the Council of State to Philip II, the Spanish ruler of Milan.[26]

MADRIGALI
A CINQUE VOCI
DI GIOSEPPE CAIMO NOBILE MILANESE
Organista nel Duomo di Milano, novamente
composti, & dati in luce.
*LIBRO QUARTO.*
IN VENETIA
Presso Giacomo Vincenzi, & Ricciardo Amadino, compagni,
MDLXXXV [Bass partbook: MDLXXXIIII]
A instantia de Pietro Tini Libraro in Milano.

Two complete copies of this collection are extant: one in the Bayerische Staatsbibliothek, Munich, and the other in the Biblioteca Estense, Modena. They appear to be identical.

Like the *Madrigali a 5,* the *Fiamma ardente* collection (RISM 1586[19]) was published by Vincenzi and Amadino "a instantia di Pietro Tini."

FIAMMA ARDENTE
DE MADRIGALI ET CANZONI

à Cinque Voci,
Con un Dialogo à Dieci de diversi soggetti, novamente
raccolte, & datte in luce, per Gio: Battista
Portio Novarese.
IN VENETIA
Presso Giacomo Vincenzi, & Ricciardo Amadino, compagni
MDLXXXVI.
A instantia di Pietro Tini.

In addition to the fourteen pieces by Caimo, the collection contains anonymous works and compositions by Michiel Varotto. Two copies of *Fiamma ardente* are known to survive: one in Biblioteca Estense, Modena, and the other in the Library of Congress, Washington, D.C.

Except for [3] "Bene mio, tu m'hai lasciato" from *Fiamma ardente,* all works in these three collections are *unica.* "Bene mio" apparently achieved some popularity in its time; it was included in two later collections, published in 1596 and 1605, respectively.[27]

## Caimo's Madrigal Style

Caimo's madrigals are representative of the style current between the innovations of Cipriano de Rore and the dramatic works of Luca Marenzio. Expanding upon the musical pictorialism of Rore's idiom, Caimo availed himself of graphic compositional devices for text portrayal while preserving the musical continuity of the composition. He was especially fond of vivid harmonic colors, moving outside of the mode through third-related progressions, chromaticism, and circle-of-fifths progressions extending as far as a G-flat major triad.

In the following section, I will treat the characteristics and development of Caimo's madrigal style as evidenced in his *Madrigali a 4* and *Madrigali a 5.* The works from *Fiamma ardente* will be treated in a separate section, since they bear resemblance to both the madrigal and canzonetta styles of the time.

### The Poetry of the Madrigali a 4

The opening work in the 1564 collection is addressed to Caimo's patron, Count Ludovico Galerato, praising the virtue, nobility, and worthy works of the count and Portia (presumably his wife). Several other texts in this collection address specific individuals. [5] "Eccelsa e generosa prole" lauds Rudolf and Ernst, the sons of Maximilian II, and bears a dedication to them. [17] "Ardir, senno, virtù" extols the virtues of Ippolita (possibly the daughter of Count Lodovico Visconti Borromeo of Milan).[28] And several poems (typical examples of *poesia per musica*) address a woman named Gratia. Such works are typically homorhythmic, allowing the text to be easily perceived.

Caimo's early madrigal collection contains numerous multipartite compositions: six madrigals in two sections, a *sestina,* and a dialogue set antiphonally for eight voices. Most of the two-section works are settings of sonnets, with the octave forming the *prima parte* and the sestet the *seconda parte.* A notable exception is [15] "Piangi, colle sacrato"–"Lagrimate, voi fiumi," a setting of twelve verses from Jacopo Sannazaro's highly popular *Arcadia.*[29] This poem is written in *terza rima,* with groups of three lines forming an interlocking rhyme scheme: *aba, bcb, cdc,* etc. Caimo selected his text from the *Arcadia's* eleventh eclogue, in which the hero, Ergasto, sings a lament at the tomb of his mother and plays on the *sampogna,* a bagpipe. (The instrument is specifically mentioned in the madrigal "E se tu, riva, udisti.") "Piangi, colle sacrato"–"Lagrimate, voi fiumi" comprises lines 4–15 of this eclogue, where Ergasto calls upon nature—its hills, caves, rivers, and sounds—to weep in sympathy with his grief.

Two other madrigals in the 1564 collection use texts from the eleventh eclogue of the *Arcadia.* [16] "Piangete, valli," the work immediately following [15] "Piangi, colle sacrato"–"Lagrimate, voi fiumi," is a setting of the next six lines in the eclogue (i.e., lines 16–21) but, interestingly, is not designated as a *terza parte.*[30] Even more surprising is the fact that the madrigal [12] "E se tu, riva, udisti," found several pages earlier than "Piangi, colle sacrato,"[31] presents the six lines that follow "Piangete, valli" in Sannazaro's text (i.e., lines 22–27). Although "Piangete, valli" and "E se tu, riva, udisti" share the same final with "Piangi, colle sacrato"–"Lagrimate, voi fiumi," the overall range of these two madrigals is lower. In spite of their noncontiguous placement in Caimo's collection, "Piangete, valli" and "E se tu, riva, udisti" are very closely related. The clef distribution is the same in both works, the voice ranges are nearly identical, and the melodic materials are similar. In fact, the motive accompanying line 2 of "Piangete, valli" is identical to the opening of "E se tu, riva, udisti."[32] Should the latter work in fact have been placed after "Piangete, valli" as its *seconda parte?*[33]

As will be shown below, Sannazaro's impassioned eclogue moved Caimo to the most expressive language of his early style. All of the madrigals from the *Arcadia* are filled with chromaticism, word painting, and striking harmonies.

The madrigal labelled *sestina* in the first book is not, in fact, a poetic sestina, but an ode by Bernardo Tasso (1493–1569), father of the more famous Torquato.[34] Although the poem does have six stanzas (presumably the reason for its being called *sestina*), it differs from the prototypical poetic form in two respects: each stanza contains only five lines, and the ending words for the individual lines are not the same in each strophe.[35] Caimo provides an independent musical setting for each of the six stanzas.

The madrigal labelled *dialogo,* on the anonymous text "Donna, l'ardente fiamma," stands as the final composition in the *Madrigali a 4.* This popular poem was set by at least nine cinquecento composers,[36] generally with the portions for the *signore* and the *donna* treated as a *prima parte* and a *seconda parte.* Caimo, however, wrote an eight-part antiphonal dialogue instead.

Among the poets represented in Caimo's early madrigals, Sannazaro appears to have been his favorite. In addition to the selections from the *Arcadia* mentioned above, the first madrigal book contains one of his sonnets. Other poets represented include Luigi Cassola,[37] Bernardo Tasso (cited above), and Alfonso d'Avalos, whose "Anchor che col partire" was immortalized by Cipriano de Rore. Caimo set the same text as Rore, but his version is lighter in tone and more chordal. At the same time, Caimo's setting makes clear reference to that of his illustrious predecessor: it adopts the rhythm of Rore's opening line, his dotted figure for the text "e cosi mill' e mille volt' il giorno" ("and thus a thousand and a thousand times a day"), and his typical repetition of the last portion of music and text, a rare feature of Caimo's early madrigals.

### The Poetry of the Madrigali a 5

Caimo's fourth madrigal book contains no dedicatory works and only three multipartite compositions: a sonnet,[38] a five-stanza canzone, and a setting of Guarini's famous "Thirsi morir volea." At the same time, several of the individual madrigals appear to be related poetically, and, at times, musically as well. For example, the first three works, "Sculpio ne l'alma Amore," "Come esser può," and "Va lieto a mort' il core" seem to be three stanzas of the same poem, set by Caimo as three individual madrigals. The texts of the three works are related in content and utilize the same rhymes and line lengths. Musically, the opening of "Va lieto a mort' il core" is clearly an ornamented version of the beginning of "Come esser può"; other correspondences in melodic figuration appear periodically throughout the three pieces.[39]

Similarly, [11] "Poi che ne' bei sospiri" is apparently the second stanza of [10] "Poi che 'l mio largo pianto," although it is not designated as such in Caimo's collection,[40] and [13] "Se voi sete il mio sol" is labelled a *risposta* to "Scoprirò l'ardor mio" in the quinto part only. The latter two poems, which share the same ending words for each line, were set by Giovanni de Castro and Giovanni Maria Nanino as *prima parte* and *seconda parte.*[41]

For his five-voiced madrigals Caimo may have taken some texts from previously published musical collections rather than directly from poetic sources. Especially interesting is the relation between his fourth book and the *Primo libro de madrigali a quattro voci* of Maddalena Casulana, which, though first published in 1568, was reprinted in 1583 (a year before Caimo's *Madrigali a 5*) at the instigation of the Milanese booksellers Francesco and Simon Tini.[42] Five poems are common to Caimo's and Casulana's collections.[43] That Caimo maintained connections with the Tini firm appears certain since Pietro Tini, successor to Francesco and Simon, promoted three of the composer's publications between 1584 and 1586.[44] If, indeed, Caimo used Casulana's 1583 print as the source for some of the texts of his 1584 madrigals, it would help to date the composition, as well as the publication, of these pieces.

Several poems in Caimo's fourth book were very popular madrigal texts of the time. In addition to Guarini's "Thirsi morir volea" (set by over two dozen composers), Caimo included Tasso's "Gel' ha madonna il core" ([5]),[45] found in at least a dozen other settings, and the anonymous "Poi che 'l mio largo pianto" ([11]), set by at least fifteen other composers.

Also included in the later madrigal collection is [9] "Mi suggean l'api il mele," a text by Girolamo Casone, whose *Rime* were not printed until after Caimo's death,[46] and two religious works, [15] "Chi mov' il piè" by Gabriel Fiamma[47] and [16] "È ben ragion," an anonymous text for Good Friday.[48] The latter moved Caimo to the most far-reaching harmonic progressions in any of his works.

## Musical Portrayal of the Poetry in Caimo's Madrigals

So striking are the musical analogs for words and phrases in the sixteenth-century madrigal style that the genre has lent its name to the phenomenon of text painting. In spite of this tradition, repetitions of short text phrases in Caimo's early madrigals are often accompanied by quite varied musical settings: the same words may be set at different speeds, in a juxtaposition of duple and triple meter, or in contrasting textures.[49] This practice obviously results in two or more rather distinctive renditions of the same words. In his later madrigals Caimo avoids such inconsistencies. While short text fragments are still often set to new music, the various renditions of a given phrase carefully preserve its emotional affect.

Syllabic settings abound in Caimo's early madrigals, possibly to avoid distracting the listener's attention from the vibrant chromatic and third-related progressions so common in these early works. In the later madrigals, melismas are far more prevalent and even serve at times as word-painting devices.

This is not to say that Caimo was insensitive to the text in his early works. On the contrary, typical madrigalisms are abundant: "sospir" ("sigh") surrounded by silence, a rest following "star" ("wait"), or a melisma for "canto" ("song").[50] In an extreme example, the end of [7] "Se potesse morir," Caimo seemingly could not resist a musical pun to illustrate the last line, "fra mille mort' io non potrei morire" ("amid a thousand deaths I could not die"). As the poet could not "die," so the composer could not properly cadence: the singers literally expire on the final chord—a semiminim on a weak part of the *tactus;* rests and *custodis* (spelling GCAD) follow, implying more to come (see plate 1).[51]

One of the most striking features of the *Madrigali a 4* is their chromaticism, consistently employed by Caimo to meet the expressive demands of the poetry. Chromatic lines play a particularly crucial role in those madrigals with texts from Sannazaro's *Arcadia*. [15] "Piangi, colle sacrato" opens with a chromatic figure coupled with suspensions to portray the weeping hills of Sannazaro's dark text.[52] A longer chromatic line, imitated in all four voices, opens [16] "Piangete, valli." In [12] "E se tu, riva, udisti," however, the motive finds its most intense expression: the phrase "la dolente sampogna a pianger volta" ("the mournful bagpipe has turned to weeping") is set to a descending chromatic figure imitatively repeated eight times, culminating at mm. 14–21 in a wonderful stretto. These pieces are without doubt the most adventurous compositions in the early madrigal collection, eliciting from Caimo the most striking language of his youthful style.

In several of his early madrigals Caimo creates stunning harmonic effects through the use of mediant progressions. Frequently accompanied by a chromatic line in one voice, these dramatic color changes underscore such words as "per duol" ("in grief") or "fredde mente" ("her cold mind").[53] These dramatic sonorities represent a deviation from the bounds of traditional modality, justified, as Vicentino explains,[54] by the text.

The five-voiced madrigals contain less overt chromaticism than the early works. Nevertheless, they demonstrate even more subtlety and agility in terms of text painting. A case in point is [16] "È ben ragion," a madrigal cited for its boldness by Einstein, Kroyer, and others.[55] Here Caimo depicts Christ's crown of thorns with tortured suspensions (mm. 20–30), "l'eterno motore" ("the eternal mover") with a sudden increase in motion, "che d'altra nebbia il mondo anco sia tinto" ("that the world also be darkened with another mist") with black notes (mm. 69–76), and "tenebroso horrore" ("dark horrors") with a low descending passage (mm. 81–84). For the portrayal of "l'empio nostro errore ha d'ogni luce il fonte, ahi lasso, estinto" ("our impious error has extinguished, alas, the fountain of all light") a chromatic line and third-related progression lead to two F-sharp major triads in close succession (mm. 60–68). Caimo renders this passage all the more striking by following it with rests in all voices. Earlier in the same work, the listener is treated to a circle-of-fifths progression leading to a G-flat major triad that is followed, in turn, by three third-related chords: B-flat major, G major, and B major (mm. 36–45). The fact that other composers such as Lasso and Marenzio had already ventured into the same tonal realms[56] dilutes Caimo's originality, but does not detract from the emotional intensity of the passage. Nor is this madrigal alone in its intriguing harmonic writing: a similarly adventurous passage may be found in [5] "Gel' ha madonna il core" (see mm. 18ff.).

The five-voiced madrigals also make increased use of *Augenmusik* and other semiotic plays on the text. Coloration exemplifies "black," "cloudy," or "dark";[57] "sol" is often either set on a G or a D, or stranded "alone" in one voice;[58] and in [17] "Cener et ombra," the last stanza of the canzone, the alto is literally abandoned by the other voices on the word "abbandonato" (see m. 20).

## Musical Texture

The early madrigal collection contains a surprising amount of homorhythm. In fact, six works are almost completely chordal throughout. Five of these six involve some form of address: a conversation, a laudatory speech to a lover, a dedicatory work, etc. In the late madrigals, homorhythm is used much more sparingly, but regularly underscores unusual harmonic progressions or changes to triple meter.

In a quarter of the late madrigals, the quinto is a second soprano, a voicing typical of the newer compositions of the time. In the remaining works, the quinto is a second tenor. Adept in his handling of the five-voiced medium, Caimo frequently varies the vocal scoring, shifting the number and distribution of voices singing at any one time. A striking example is the solo opening of "Cener et ombra" ([17], part 5), which is followed by complete silence before the entrance of the other parts. This dramatic textural contrast not only creates variety, but also vividly illustrates the lonely emptiness of the poet's life.

Caimo often treats the five voices of these late madrigals as a single unit rather than as individual independent lines. Unlike the early works, every voice need not state the entire text. In [2] "Come esser può," for example, the canto appropriately rests on the words "sepolto" ("buried"), "more" ("die"), and "morte" ("death").

## Musical Form

Repetition of musical sections is far more common in Caimo's late madrigals than in his earlier ones. In book 4 nine pieces contain textual and musical repeats of the last two to four lines; in book 1, however,

only two pieces do—[11] "Anchor che col partire" and [6] "Chi vuol veder in terra." In both cases Caimo was seemingly influenced by previous settings of the same texts that contained repeated sections at or near their ends. We have noted above the many similarities between Caimo's "Anchor che col partire" and Rore's famous setting of this poem. In the case of "Chi vuol veder in terra," Caimo seems to have consulted the earlier setting by Pietro Taglia (who may have been his teacher),[59] although Caimo changes Taglia's "Laura" to "Gratia." Just as he did with Rore's madrigal, Caimo demonstrates his cognizance of Taglia's earlier setting by emulating its closing strategy. Thus in Taglia's madrigal, the last two lines of text and music are repeated, then followed by a brief "coda" that restates the last line in triple meter. Like Taglia, Caimo changes from duple to triple meter for the final statement of the last line. He then repeats the entire concluding section, encompassing the final two lines of the poem. In addition to similarities in formal structure, the two madrigals contain striking correspondences in rhythmic figuration in several places.[60]

## Metric Structure

Caimo's two madrigal books reflect a common trend of the era, the increasing use of the meter sign C in preference to ₵. While all of the 1564 works use ₵, every piece except one in the later collection is written *a note nere* (a term derived from the shorter—and therefore "blacker"—notes associated with C). The single exception in the 1584 collection is [6] "Thirsi morir volea," which is written *alla breve*. In spite of its ₵ signature, the note values in this piece are not significantly longer than those of the other works in the book. In fact, Caimo even uses *fusae* to mimic "trembling eyes" and to illustrate Guarini's final maxim that "in order to die again, they came back to life." Why Caimo chose ₵ for this work remains unclear. Might this piece provide support for Einstein's theory that by this time ₵ was considered "a measure of pathos" used "to express extreme states of temperamental distress"?[61]

## Summary

Comparison of the two volumes of madrigals reveals significant developments in Caimo's compositional style, documenting the growth of a highly creative young composer into a "master of pathos."[62] Although most of these developments have been noted in the analysis above, they are, for convenience of comparison, summarized here. Caimo's late madrigals differ from his early works in the following ways:

1. The poetry is freer in form and many of the texts contain stronger emotional contrasts, juxtapos-

ing, for example, "vita" and "morte," "gelo" and "fiamma," "pianto" and "canto."[63] This development reflects the general change in literary fashion from the pastorals of Sannazaro and the odes of Bernardo Tasso to the new lyric verse of Torquato Tasso and Guarini.

2. There are no dedicatory works.

3. There are fewer multisection compositions, although several individual pieces are related poetically and a few of them were set as two-section madrigals by other composers.

4. When text phrases within a particular work are repeated, the musical settings tend to be similar in emotional affect. This practice contrasts sharply with Caimo's earlier style in which the same text is often set in contrasting meters, textures, or tempos.

5. The late works contain less chromaticism, but more adventurous harmonic language, more literal word painting, and more *Augenmusik*.

6. The text setting tends to be more melismatic.

7. There is much less homorhythm.

8. There is a greater amount of sectional repetition.

9. There is increased use of C over ₵.

Several of these developments (e.g., nos. 1 and 9) are characteristic of changes in the sixteenth-century madrigal in general. A number of them, however (e.g., nos. 4, 5, and 6), appear to reflect growth in Caimo's personal approach to the madrigal form.

## The Compositions from *Fiamma ardente*

The fourteen pieces by Caimo in the collection *Fiamma ardente* show the composer's attempts (typical at the time) to reconcile the canzonetta style with the more elevated madrigal. Caimo's success in this endeavor is shown by the popularity of at least one of the works in the collection, "Bene mio, tu m'hai lasciato," which, as noted above, was reprinted in several collections published after the composer's death.

In his preface to the *Fiamma ardente* collection, Giovanni Battista Portio calls Caimo's works "napolitane canzoni."[64] Indeed, these works are in a lighter vein than Caimo's madrigals, particularly in terms of the poetry. Unlike typical madrigal texts, the poems in this collection are extremely short and often frivolous. Many contain the similes with nature typical of the popular genre: "I would I were a bee,"[65] "My heart has become an Aetna," etc. The works show similarities to the canzonetta style in their use of sectional repetition, their restrained text painting, and their extensive use of homophony (more pronounced here than in the late madrigals, but still not as prevalent as in the *Madrigali a 4*).

In spite of Portio's appellation, however, the *Fiamma ardente* compositions owe a great deal to the madrigal style. Even the poems were not always distinguished by composers of the time as belonging entirely to one genre or the other. Several of the texts Caimo chose were set by other composers as madrigals,[66] and in three cases the same poem appears in a volume of "canzoni" or "canzonette" by one composer and in a volume of madrigals by another.[67] In the tradition of the madrigal, Caimo set only single strophes or presented independent musical settings for each stanza of a poem. This practice stands in contrast to the typical strophic form of the canzonetta. The collection contains two multipartite works: a four-section canzone and Torquato Tasso's "Vola, vola, pensier," which is followed by a *risposta*, "Torna, torna, pensier," set entirely for high voices.[68] The use of five voices and the significant amount of text repetition also derive from the madrigal style, making the musical structure of these compositions more complex than that of Caimo's canzonette. Although the poems themselves are short, the amount of text repetition in these pieces makes them as long as or longer than Caimo's madrigals.

Sectional repeats are characteristic of nearly all the works. Of the single-strophe pieces, six repeat the last line of text and music and one the first line; two are set in the form AABB, and one uses the structure AABCC. For the multistrophic texts, Caimo varies the formal setting with each stanza. In the canzone, for example, part 1 repeats the last line only; the other strophes use variants of the form AABB. In the third stanza only half of section B is repeated (with some variants), and in the fourth a small coda follows the second repeat. Similarly, in the two-part "Vola, vola, pensier" the first stanza repeats line one, but the second is through-composed.

Caimo's musical settings can hardly be compared to the crude *canzone villanesca alla napolitana* of the first half of the century, with its unsophisticated harmonic language and frequent use of parallel fifths.[69] At the same time, the pieces generally resemble the canzonetta more than the madrigal in their harmonic language: melodic chromaticism does not play a large role, and third-related progressions, so common in both of Caimo's madrigal books, are rare. Though contemporaneous with his late madrigals, these more popular works do not venture into the exotic harmonic realms Caimo explored in his fourth madrigal book.

The lack of text painting in the *Fiamma ardente* works is well illustrated by [3] "Bene mio, tu m'hai lasciato," in which the same lively figure portraying "bene mio" ("my love") at the beginning is used for "morirò" ("I shall die") in m. 21. In fact, the same melodic motive appears for the onomatopoeic "tic e toc" in another work, [7] "Lo core mio." On the other hand, Caimo the madrigalist did not resist *fusae* for "mormorando" ("murmuring"), long notes and suspensions for "l'aspro mio dolore" ("my harsh sorrow"), a call-and-response texture for "rispose" ("replied"), and a slippery succession of suspensions for "per inganni" ("by deception").[70]

## Editorial Procedures

### Sources

Except for [3] "Bene mio, tu m'hai lasciato" from *Fiamma ardente*, the publications described under Compositions and Sources are the only surviving sources for Caimo's madrigals. Variant readings from the Phalèse and Haestens publications of "Bene mio, tu m'hai lasciato" are cited in the Critical Commentary.

### Note Values

Note values are halved in transcription. The sign ₵ has been retained in this edition; C has been rendered as $\frac{2}{4}$. Time signature changes on the staff are generally editorial and have therefore been enclosed in square brackets. Occasionally, a time signature change is reproduced from the original, in which case it appears without brackets. Final notes have been rendered as whole notes regardless of their notation in the original prints. (Final notes in the *Madrigali a 4* are breves with fermatas; final notes in other sources are longs.) Rest values are also halved, except that empty measures are given whole rests in accordance with modern convention.

### Accidentals

In conformity with the aims of a practical edition, the present collection adopts the modern convention in which an accidental on the staff applies to all succeeding notes of the same pitch within one measure. At the same time, the edition aims to serve the scholar of Renaissance music by providing all information needed to reconstruct the original sources.

Ordinary accidentals on the staff are explicit in the source. Small accidentals on the staff are not explicit, but are implied by the conventions of the source (see "Musica Ficta" below). Accidentals in parentheses on the staff are cautionary, warning the performer against potential errors caused by inflections in other voices or in close proximity within the same voice.

Accidentals above the notes are suggested by the editor in accordance with policies given below under "Musica Ficta." When a note affected by a previous accidental on the staff has the same accidental above it, the source does not specify that accidental explicitly or imply it by convention. Thus, all accidentals

supplied by the editor and only accidentals supplied by the editor are found above the staff.

### Musica Ficta

The two publishers of Caimo's works adopted very different editorial procedures regarding the notation of accidentals. In Moscheni's 1564 print of the *Madrigali a 4*, accidentals pertain only to the note immediately following; in the two publications by Vincenzi and Amadino (the *Madrigali a 5* and *Fiamma ardente*), however, an accidental preceding the first of several repeated notes generally applies to all of them.[71] This difference in style between the early and late works probably reflects the preferences of the two publishers and should not be taken as a general chronological trend.

It follows that in the 1564 print, successive inflected notes on the same pitch all bear explicit accidentals. The accidental is repeated both when there is an intervening rest (over twenty-five instances) and when the repetition occurs without a rest (over eighty instances). At times there are three or more accidentals in a row (e.g., p. 54, mm. 34–35, tenor, where the natural sign is repeated in the print on four successive notes—see plate 2). This practice in itself should be sufficient to suggest that when an accidental is not repeated, it should not be retained. In addition, however, there are numerous cases in which perfect consonances in the harmonic structure confirm that an uninflected note following an inflected one must be natural. For examples with an intervening rest, see p. 20, mm. 21–22, tenor, and p. 17, m. 19, canto (where a subsequent change of bass in m. 20 confirms the c″-natural at the end of m. 19). Examples without an intervening rest present more of a problem. However, there are more than a dozen instances in the context of a changing harmony in which the second note must be natural. See, for example, p. 43, m. 14, where the c-natural in the bass is confirmed by octaves and fifths in the tenor and the canto. The tenor's c′-natural is further supported by the f's in the alto and bass in the next measure. The last two f's in the bass in m. 15 bear explicit sharps in the source. It is clear, however, that the f's at the beginning of mm. 15 and 16 must both be sung as natural in view of the perfect consonances in the other parts.

When the harmony is stable, the interpretation becomes more questionable. However, the reader should examine p. 74, mm. 1–4, where the chromatic lines in the upper parts are confirmed by the bass, which is compelled to move chromatically by perfect consonances in the other parts. In other cases, the beginning of a new phrase on the uninflected second note suggests that the accidental should not be retained (e.g., p. 16, m. 8, alto). Such situations resemble those in which a rest intervenes between the repeated pitches. In still other cases, melodic parallels suggest that the accidental should apply only to the note immediately following (e.g., p. 74, mm. 1–3, canto, alto, and tenor).

Although one finds occasions in Renaissance sources when an accidental on the second of two repeated notes must be applied retroactively to the first one as well,[72] the weight of the evidence in Caimo's publications suggests that this practice is not applicable here. In over twenty-five instances with a changing bass, the context confirms that the first note must remain uninflected (e.g., p. 16, m. 10, alto). Once again, where the bass remains stable, the situation is more questionable. In view of the very strong evidence that accidentals in this collection are intended to apply only to the note immediately following, the editor has been cautious about suggesting additional musica ficta in such places. In cases such as pp. 13 and 14, mm. 11 and 19, however, it is tempting to assume errors in the print and suggest b′-flats in the canto on the pitches preceding the notated accidental. Such cases are treated in the Critical Commentary below.

The immediate juxtaposition of an inflected pitch with an uninflected one also appears frequently between two voices, creating a cross relation—a practice James Haar has shown to be common in the mid-sixteenth-century madrigal.[73] In fact, Caimo's 1564 print alone contains nearly two dozen cross relations, most of which can be confirmed as intentional by perfect consonances in other parts (e.g., p. 4, m. 11, tenor to canto). The majority of these cross relations involve a sharped note at the cadence followed by an uninflected one at the beginning of the next phrase (e.g., p. 67, m. 8). In two cases, one in the *Madrigali a 4* and one in the *Madrigali a 5,* the uninflected note at the beginning of the new phrase actually overlaps the sharped note at the end of the previous one (see p. 10, m. 5, and pp. 94–95, mm. 39 and 64). Although Don Harrán would probably consider these sharps cautionary, warning the performer *not* to sharp the pitch (see note 72), the frequency of cross relations between phrases in Caimo's madrigals suggests that these two cases are oversights that may have resulted from adding the cadential sharp while proofreading the music in partbook format. The editor recommends that in these cases the sharped note should merely be shortened rhythmically.

In spite of Moscheni's care in indicating every necessary accidental in the 1564 print, there are nevertheless a few omissions. Seven such errors are indisputable (e.g., p. 53, m. 13, where all but one of the ten e's in the tenor and bass bear explicit flats in the source—see plate 2). A similar number of instances are debatable; all are discussed in the Critical Com-

mentary. All things considered, however, the number of errors in this print is miniscule in relation to the hundreds of notated accidentals.

Unlike Moscheni, the publishers of Caimo's late works generally adopted a policy in which an explicit accidental pertains to succeeding repeated notes unless a rest intervenes. The reader may note, for example, page 106, mm. 19–22, where only two of the f's in the alto are marked with sharps, but it is clear that the remaining ones should be inflected as well, in view of the B's in the bass and canto and the explicit C-sharps and F-sharps in the canto, quinto, tenor, and bass (see plate 4). Similarly, in the tenor, the sharp only appears before the first c′ in m. 22, but clearly should carry into m. 23, as F-sharps, C-sharps, and G-sharps are specified in other voices.[74] It is instructive to compare this madrigal (bk. 4, no. 5) with "E se tu, riva, udisti" (bk. 1, no. 12); in the latter (p. 62) the F-natural in m. 19, bass, and the C-naturals in m. 14, alto, and m. 18, bass, are clearly required by octaves in the other voices, resulting in chromatic melodic lines (see plate 3).

The practice of a single accidental affecting a succession of repeated notes is so clear in Caimo's late works that the addition of editorial accidentals in these cases becomes superfluous. In fact, adding such accidentals implies that they are suggestions on the part of the present editor rather than the intentions of the original publishers. To do so would, moreover, be to apply the editorial policy of Moscheni to the very different practices of Vincenzi and Amadino.

In summary, then, to reconstruct the 1564 print, the reader should replace tacit accidentals with explicit ones unless stated otherwise in the Critical Commentary. To reconstruct the later prints, replace tacit accidentals only where rests or different pitches intervene between explicit accidentals and the notes that by modern convention would immediately be affected.

Editorial accidentals have been supplied at full cadences. For avoided cadences accidentals have generally been suggested if the sixth to octave or third to unison appears in two voices.[75] Horizontal tritones have also been eliminated by the addition of ficta. Vertical tritones have occasionally been allowed to stand unchanged when one of the notes is passing or unaccented and when one or both pitches resolve correctly according to the contrapuntal practice of the time. Other standard rules of musica ficta, such as "una nota supra la," have been invoked when applicable. In addition, editorial accidentals have been added without comment to eliminate melodic augmented seconds and to render the final chord of each piece major.[76] Situations subject to differing interpretations are treated in the Critical Commentary.

### Texts

Text underlay follows the principles set forth by Zarlino and Vicentino. Spellings changed from those in the original prints and errors corrected in this edition are acknowledged in "Notes on the Text" in Texts and Translations. Accents have been modernized and appropriate punctuation added. Where spellings vary among the voice parts, the one used in the majority of parts has been adopted. If the parts show variant spellings with equal frequency, the more modern spelling is used. Ampersands have been realized as *e* or *et* (*ed* never appears in these prints). The beginning of a text line is capitalized the first time it appears; repetitions of the line are not capitalized unless another text line intervenes.[77] Angle brackets enclose text repetitions indicated in the original print by *ij* or *·//·*; square brackets surround editorial additions of text. The author of the text, when known, is cited at the head of the piece in the upper left corner. The original prints furnish no names of authors. The poetic sources consulted for the present edition are cited in Texts and Translations.

### Titles, Sectional Headings, and Attributions

Unless otherwise indicated in the Critical Commentary, titles of works are given as they appear in the tables of contents of the original prints, but accents have been modernized, punctuation added, and errors corrected. Spellings conform to the version established in Texts and Translations.

Sectional headings such as *prima* and *seconda parte*, *risposta*, etc. appear in the original prints, either at the beginning of a new section (*Madrigali a 5* and *Fiamma ardente*) or sometimes at the end of the previous section (*Madrigali a 4*). The generic terms *sestina, canzone*, etc. appear either on the music pages or in the tables of contents of the original prints.

In madrigal collections that also contain the works of other composers, Caimo's name appears above the music for each of his pieces.

### Other Editorial Procedures

In this edition, only the treble clef (𝄞), the transposed treble clef (𝄞), and the bass clef (𝄢) are used. Original clefs are given in incipits. The alto voice generally uses the treble clef but is occasionally given with the transposed treble clef when the range so demands. For the five-voiced works, the quinto is sometimes placed below the canto and sometimes below the alto, depending on its range. For multisection madrigals, no new incipit is given unless there is a change of clef in the original. Range finders are provided for each section, however. A continuous overhead bracket ( ⎯ ) indicates a ligature, a broken overhead bracket ( ⌐ ¬ ), coloration.

## Acknowledgments

I would particularly like to thank Prof. James Haar and Christopher Hill, my editor at A-R Editions, for their careful reading of my manuscript and for their perceptive comments and suggestions. Special thanks are also due the following scholars for their help and advice during the preparation of this edition: Profs. Karol Berger, Anna Maria Busse Berger, Robert Durling, William Mahrt, Anthony Newcomb, Jessie Ann Owens, and Imanuel Willheim. I am also grateful for the funding provided by the University of California, Santa Cruz (UCSC), and the help and cooperation of the staffs of the following libraries: the British Library; the Library of Congress; the Bayerische Staatsbibliothek, Munich; University of California, Berkeley; UCSC; Harvard; Yale; and the Folger Shakespeare Library.

# Notes

1. Alfred Einstein, *The Italian Madrigal*, trans. Alexander H. Krappe, Roger H. Sessions, and Oliver Strunk (Princeton, N.J.: Princeton University Press, 1949; preface dated 1943), 561.

2. H. Simonsfeld, "Mailänder Briefe zur bayerischen und allgemeinen Geschichte des 16. Jahrhunderts," in *Abhandlungen der Historischen Classe der Königlich, bayerischen Akademie der Wissenschaften*, 22 (Munich: Verlag der K. Akademie, 1902), 335 (letter 158, Prospero Visconti to Duke William, 14 July 1574).

3. Ibid., 290 (letter 79, Prospero Visconti to Duke William, 25 November 1572).

4. *Il secondo libro di canzonette a quattro voci* (Venice: Giacomo Vincenzi and Ricciardo Amadino, 1584). The preface by Pietro Tini refers to "l'acerba, et impensata morte del buon M. Gioseppe Caimo, Musico, et organista del duomo

di Milano." G. B. Portio's preface to the madrigal collection *Fiamma ardente,* dated 1 December 1585, mentions Gioseppe Caimo "della felice memoria." The death date of 1588—given by Gustave Reese, *Music in the Renaissance,* 2d ed. (New York: W. W. Norton, 1958), 432, and several other sources—is based on Damiano Muoni, *Gli Antignati organari insigni e serie dei maestri di cappella del duomo di Milano* (Milan, 1883; reprint, Bologna: Forni, [1969]), 25, wherein are listed the organists with their dates of employment. Caimo is designated as holding the position from 1580; the next organist mentioned is Gaspare Costa in 1588. Muoni's information may come from *Annali della fabbrica del duomo di Milano dall' origine fino al presente* (Milan: G. Brigola, 1877–85). Dates of appointments for organists are not given in this work, but Caimo is cited twice in 1580 for receiving salary increases (vol. 4, p. 176). The next mention of any organist is Costa in 1588.

5. See also Patricia Brauner, "Giuseppe Caimo, 'Nobile Milanese' (ca. 1540–1584)," (Ph.D. diss., Yale University, 1969), ii.

6. "Mi trovo quì un organista, huomo di molta qualità in quella professione e nelli costumi." See R. Casimiri, "Paolo Bellasio, musicista Veronese (1554–1594)," *Note d'archivio per la storia musicale* 14, no. 3 (1937): 104. The only reason Borromeo would have considered replacing Caimo was that the composer was not an ecclesiastic. See Lewis Lockwood, *The Counter-Reformation and the Masses of Vincenzo Ruffo* ([Vienna]: Universal Editions, 1970), 111. Borromeo himself died on 3 November 1584. For another connection between Caimo and Borromeo, see note 28.

7. It is uncertain when Gaspare Costa assumed the position of organist at the duomo. Publications in 1580, 1581, and 1584 describe him as "organista alla Madonna di San Celso in Milano." In his canzonette of 1588, however, he is identified as "organista nel duomo di Milano."

8. Brauner's statement that Caimo had not yet received the post of organist at S. Ambrogio in 1564 is apparently an error. See Brauner, "Caimo," 42.

9. Maximilian II (1527–76) became Holy Roman Emperor in 1564. His two sons (aged ten and eleven) visited Milan on 29 December 1563, according to "Il diario di Giambattista Casale," in *Memorie storiche della diocesi di Milano,* vol. 12 (Milan: Biblioteca Ambrosiana, 1965), 220. Caimo's "Eccelsa e generosa prole," included in the *Madrigali a 4,* was apparently written in honor of the event. Contrary to a statement in *The New Grove Dictionary of Music and Musicians,* s.v. "Caimo, Gioseppe," by Iain Fenlon, this piece is not the first work in Caimo's collection.

10. See Simonsfeld, "Mailänder Briefe," nos. 38, 79, 127, 129, 157, 158, 205, and 206. William V ruled Bavaria from the time of his father's death in 1579 until 1597.

11. Ibid., 335 (letter 158, Prospero Visconti to Duke William, 14 July 1574).

12. "Una fuga, che V.S. le darà, et ancora alla riversa et doppia et farla sentire molte volte con tutte le parti." Ibid., 357 (letter 206, Prospero Visconti to Duke Ferdinand, 1 October 1575). Visconti wrote to both Duke William and Duke Ferdinand on this day in anticipation of Caimo's visit to the court. See ibid., 356–57 (letters 205 and 206).

13. "Un raro virtuoso con la mano assai gagliarda e velocissima." Ibid.

14. Both Caimo and Vicentino were paid ten crowns. See ibid., 263 (letter 38, Gasparo Visconti to Duke William, 14 December 1570).

15. Ibid., 335 (letter 158; see note 11).

16. Ibid., 356 (letter 205, Prospero Visconti to Duke William, 1 October 1575).

17. Ibid., 263. See also Henry Kaufmann, *The Life and Works of Nicola Vicentino* (n.p.: American Institute of Musicology, 1966), 41–42, 46. Caimo may also be one of the two musicians recommended for the duke's service in a letter from Hans Fugger in Augsburg on 29 January 1574. See Kaufmann, *Vicentino,* 46.

18. Kaufmann, *Vicentino,* 42, 46–47; and Lockwood, *Counter-Reformation,* 95. In a letter of 25 March 1570, Vicentino describes himself as rector of St. Thomas's, Milan. In 1571 and 1572 his fourth and fifth books of motets were published there. There is evidence that he was residing in the city shortly before his death, supervising the construction of an arcicembalo.

19. *Annali della fabbrica del duomo di Milano* 4:176.

20. Ibid.

21. Lockwood, *Counter-Reformation,* 57. The maestro at this time was Pietro Ponzio, who served in that capacity from 1577 to 1582. Arcangelo de Gani, *I maestri cantori e la cappella musicali del Duomo di Milano dalle origini al presente* (Milan: E. Cattaneo, 1930), states that Ponzio remained at the duomo until 1588.

22. The bass part of the *Madrigali a 5* bears the date 1584, but the other four parts read 1585.

23. Brauner, "Caimo," and Fenlon, "Caimo," state that there are eighteen pieces because they are considering each portion of the multisectional works separately.

24. "Volendo mandar in publico questi Madrigali miei, frutti veramente immaturi delli miei mal coltivati orti; hò preso ardire di appenderli alla honorata imagine della grandezza di V. S. non gia in racompenso di veruna parte degli infiniti oblighi, quali per molte & molte honeste ragioni hò a lei: ma accio che illustrati dalla chiarezza del suo honorato nome, molto piu di favor, si arrechano. Piacciavi dunque Illustre Signor mio, accettargli con quella solita sua benignità: con la quali i cuori di tutti strettamente a se si lega." On Ludovico Galerato, see Kaufmann, *Vicentino,* 86, and Johann Heinrich Zedler, *Grosses vollständiges Universal-Lexicon aller Wissenschaften und Kunst* (Halle and Leipzig: J. H. Zedler, 1732–50; reprint Graz: Akademische Druck-U. Verlagsanstalt, 1961). The music publisher Moscheni was originally from Bergamo but published in Milan from 1541 until 1566, at first with his brothers and later alone. Both the four- and five-voiced madrigals of Pietro Taglia, who may have been Caimo's teacher, were published by this firm (in 1555 and 1557, respectively). See Claudio Sartori, *Dizionario degli editori musicali italiani* (Florence: Leo Olschki, 1958), 106.

25. The two printers jointly published seventy-six music books during the years 1583–86. After 1586 they worked separately. Many of their books were commissioned by other printers or booksellers; in the case of Caimo, the *Madrigali a 5* were published "a instantia di Pietro Tini," bookseller in Milan. Tini also promoted the publication of Caimo's four-voiced canzonette and the *Fiamma ardente* collection. For further information on Tini, see Sartori, *Dizionario,* 154.

26. For the colorful career of Perez (1534–1611), see the entry in the *Enciclopedia italiana di scienze, lettere ed arti,* s.v. "Perez, Antonio" by Angela Valente.

27. Pietro Phalesio (Pierre Phalèse), *Paradiso musicale di madrigali et canzoni a cinque voci* (Antwerp, 1596) [RISM 1596[10]] and Henrico Lodowico de' Haestens, *Nervi d'Orfeo di eccellentiss. autori a cinque et sei voci* (Leiden, 1605) [RISM 1605[9]].

28. Ippolita, the second daughter of Conte Lodovico Visconti Borromeo, was the wife of Marcantonio Dal Verme (d. 1538). The text of "Ardir, senno, virtù" makes reference

to "del vermo l'Idea." Caimo clearly had some connection to the Dal Verme family, since his canzonette of 1584 are dedicated to "Marc' Antonio Dal Verme, Conte di Zavatarello, Rovigo, e Tribecco, Signor della Torre degl' Alberi, & de Signori di Preda Gavina." The dedication apparently refers to Ippolita's grandson (1556–1632), also named Marcantonio, who was, incidentally, a distant cousin of S. Carlo Borromeo. For the connection between Caimo and Borromeo, see p. vii and note 6 above. Ippolita herself was probably born around 1500 as her first child was born in 1517. See P. Litta, *Famiglie celebri italiane,* fasc. 19, *Dal Verme di Verona* (Milan, 1831), table 3, and fasc. 9, *Visconti di Milano,* pt. 3 (Milan, 1827), table 12. There is no reason to assume, as Brauner has ("Caimo," 163), that the canzonette dedication is a joke. Except for Rovigo, the towns mentioned in the dedication are not far from Milan. Zavatarello, Trebecco (= Tribecco), Torre degl' Alberi, and Pietragavina (= Preda Gavina) lie close together in an area about 70 km south of Milan; Rovigo is in the Veneto. I am grateful to Prof. James Haar for his suggestions about the canzonette dedication, which led to my discovery of Caimo's connection to the Dal Verme family.

29. Sannazaro (1456–1530) completed the first ten eclogues of the *Arcadia* by 1489, a copyist's date on one of the manuscripts. These ten were published in 1502, and the last two eclogues were added in an edition of 1504. The work's popularity was such that new editions appeared approximately every two years. See Jacopo Sannazaro, *Arcadia and Piscatorial Eclogues,* trans. Ralph Nash (Detroit: Wayne State University Press, 1966), and William J. Kennedy, *Jacopo Sannazaro and the Uses of Pastoral* (Hanover, N.H.: The University Press of New England, 1983). The only other two-section work in Caimo's collection that is not a sonnet is "Chi vuol veder in terra," which was also set to music by the aforementioned Pietro Taglia.

30. The notation in Emil Vogel, Alfred Einstein, François Lesure, and Claudio Sartori, *Bibliografia della musica italiana vocale profana* (Geneva: Minkoff, 1977), 297, that "Piangete, valli" is part 3 of "Piangi, colle sacrato" is an error. In this work Caimo's first name is consistently given as "Giuseppi," even though it is listed in all of his publications as "Gioseppe."

31. This work appears on p. 21; "Piangi, colle sacrato" is on p. 24.

32. Cf. "Piangete, valli," mm. 5 ff., with the opening of "E se tu, riva, udisti." The use of the same motive in both works helps to solve a musica ficta problem in "Piangete, valli." See the Critical Commentary.

33. Interestingly, the six lines of "E se tu, riva, udisti" do not end with a completed sentence but require the next three to complete the thought. See Texts and Translations.

34. Bernardo Tasso became governor of Ostiglia while serving Guglielmo Gonzaga, duke of Mantua.

35. A poetic sestina has six-line stanzas; the words ending the lines of stanza 1 are repeated in succeeding strophes, but are transposed in order.

36. Caimo's is one of the earliest settings.

37. "Se potesse morir" was published in *Madrigali del Magnifico Sig. Cavallier Luigi Cassola Piacentino* (Venice: Gabriel Giolito de Ferrar', 1544). Caimo's version of the text is corrupt; see note in Texts and Translations.

38. "Chi mov' il piè" is from Gabriel Fiamma's *Rime spirituali* (Venice, 1560).

39. Cf., for example, "Sculpio ne l'alma Amore," mm. 47–49 and "Come esser può," mm. 24–26.

40. The two poems are obviously related in both structure and content (see Texts and Translations). Both poems

were also set by Pietro Vinci in 1583 (see Vogel et al., *Bibliografia,* no. 2910).

41. See Vogel et al., *Bibliografia,* no. 509, and Emil Vogel, *Bibliothek der gedruckten weltlichen Vocalmusik italiens. Aus den Jahren 1500–1700 . . . mit Nachträgen von Prof. Alfred Einstein* (Hildesheim: Georg Olms, 1972), 699, no. 1583².

42. The original publication is listed in Vogel et al., *Bibliografia,* no. 513: Maddalena Casulana de Mezari, *Primo libro de madrigali a quattro voci* (Venice: Girolamo Scotto, 1568). Only the tenor part survives today. The later printing (Vogel, no. 514) was issued in Brescia by Vincenzo Sabbio "ad instantia di Francesco, et Simon Tini, fratelli, librari in Milano, 1583." The canto and tenor parts are extant.

43. "Sculpio ne l'alma Amore," "Come esser può," "Va lieto a mort' il core," "Vedesti, Amor, giamai," and "Se voi set' il mio cor." There are a few minor variants between Caimo's texts and those of Casulana. Although only the canto and tenor parts of Casulana's *Primo libro* survive (see note 42), several of her pieces were also published in Girolamo Scotto's *Primo libro de diversi eccellentissimi autori* in 1566, which exists in a complete form today. Included in this collection are two concordances with Caimo: "Vedesti, Amor, giamai" and "Sculpio ne l'alma Amore." Casulana's madrigals are published in a modern edition by Beatrice Pescerelli, *I madrigali di Maddalena Casulana* (Florence: Leo S. Olschki, 1979). On the Tini brothers, see Sartori, *Dizionario,* 154 and note 25 above.

44. See note 25 above.

45. Tasso's original reads "Gelo ha madonna il seno."

46. *Rime del Signor Girolamo Casone, da Oderzo* (Venice: Gio. Battista Ciotti, 1598). See Gian-Giuseppe Liruti, *Notizie delle vite ed opere scritte da' letterati del Friuli* (Venice: Tipografia Alvisopoli, 1830), 241–42.

47. Fiamma, *Rime spirituali,* sonnet 80.

48. See Einstein, *Italian Madrigal,* 562.

49. See, for example, p. 32, mm. 18ff.

50. See [13] "Andate, o miei sospiri," m. 4, alto; [8] "Non consentir" (Sestina, part 4), mm. 9–11; [10] "Li vostr' occhi," m. 16; and [8] "China le sant' orecchie" (Sestina, part 6), mm. 5–6, tenor.

51. It is possible that Caimo knew Rore's "Amor, ben mi credevo" (pub. 1550), at the end of which first the canto and then the tenor drop out to illustrate the poet's extinguished life. See Bernhard Meier, ed., *Cipriani Rore opera omnia* (Rome: American Institute of Musicology, 1969), 4:28–30. The first line of Caimo's piece is erroneously given as "Se potesse mirar" in the print.

52. Caimo repeats the same melodic figure in the bass at the beginning of part 2, "Lagrimate, voi fiumi."

53. See [2] "Ma 'l cor che stava," mm. 18–19, and [8] "Scalda col tuo valore" (Sestina, part 3), m. 15.

54. In his *L'antica musica ridotta alla moderna prattica* Vicentino specifically states that in compositions such as madrigals the rules of modal composition may be broken for the sake of the text. See the discussion in Kaufmann, *Vicentino,* 208. On particularly emotional words, Vicentino allows that "one can compose every sort of step and harmony, and go outside the mode, and govern oneself according to the subject of the vernacular text" (Kaufmann, *Vicentino,* 208; Vicentino, fol. 48: "Sopra tali parole si potrà comporre ogni sorte de gradi, & di armonia, & andar fuore di Tono & reggersi secondo il suggietto delle parole volgari").

55. See Einstein, *Italian Madrigal,* 562, and Theodor Kroyer, *Die Anfänge der Chromatik im italienischen Madrigal des XVI. Jahrhunderts* (Leipzig: Breitkopf & Härtel, 1902), 128–29.

56. Lasso, in his *Prophetiae Sibyllarum,* utilized F-sharp

major triads in the "Carmina chromatico" and the "Sibylla Hellespontiaca" (see Orlando Lasso, *Prophetiae Sibyllarum, Das Chorwerk 48* (Wolfenbüttel: Möseler, [1938?]), p. 5, m. 14, and p. 17, mm. 3 and 4). In Marenzio's famous setting of Petrarch's "O voi che sospirate" (*Il secondo libro de madrigali a cinque voci*, 1581; Vogel et al., *Bibliografia*, no. 1608), the composer writes a G-flat in the bass simultaneously with an F-sharp in the alto, possibly to exemplify the words *antico stile* with a reference to the Greek enharmonic genera. See Luca Marenzio, *Sämtliche Werke*, vol. 1, Publikationen älterer Musik 4, pt. 1 (Leipzig: Breitkopf & Härtel, 1929), 69–70.

57. See, for example, [16] "È ben ragion," mm. 69ff., and [8] "Parto da voi," mm. 52ff.

58. See [12] "Se voi sete il mio sol," mm. 3ff.; [17] "O sola, o senza par" (Canzone, part 1), beginning; [3] "Valieto a mort' il core," m. 32; and [8] "Parto da voi," m. 63.

59. See Einstein, *The Italian Madrigal*, 562, and Brauner, "Caimo," x.

60. Compare Caimo's setting, part 2, mm. 9–11, with Taglia, part 2, mm. 12–15; and Caimo, part 2, m. 18, with Taglia, part 2, m. 19. Taglia's madrigals are currently being edited by Jessie Ann Owens and are due to be published by Garland Press. I am grateful to Prof. Owens for providing me with a copy of the original print of the Taglia work.

61. Einstein, *Italian Madrigal*, 470.

62. See note 1, above.

63. Examples include [5] "Gel' ha madonna il core," [7] "Io piansi un tempo," and [12] "Se voi sete il mio sol."

64. Portio claimed that some works were given to him by Caimo before his death and that others were collected from friends. "Venutomi donque alle mani le napolitane canzoni della felice memoria del S. Gioseppi Caimo musico . . . eccellentissimo, parte à me donate dall'istesso Signore, mentre viveva, & parte raccolte d'altri amici à i quali egli ne fece copia."

65. The poem, "Un' ape esser vorei" is attributed to Torquato Tasso in Vogel et al., *Bibliografia*, 3:99 and collections no. 492, 1356, 1785, and 2922. However, apparently only the first line is taken from him. See Angelo Solerti, *Le rime di Torquato Tasso*, vol. 2 (Bologna: Romagnoli-Dall'Acqua, 1898), 512.

66. For example, "Questa crudel" by Orazio Scaletta in 1585.

67. For example, [3] "Bene mio, tu m'hai lasciato" is included in volumes of madrigals by both Ippolito Baccusi and Benedetto Pallavicino (1587) and in volumes of "canzoni" or "canzonette" by Giovanni Piccioni (1582) and Paolo Quagliati (1588). [4] "Un' ape esser vorei" and [8] "Vola, vola, pensier" similarly bear conflicting designations.

68. Although labelled *risposta* in the music, the text of "Torna, torna, pensier," does not "respond" to the first stanza. See Texts and Translations.

69. Although Caimo was obviously well grounded in contrapuntal techniques, there is one case of parallel fifths in [1] "Mirate che m'ha fatto" (see m. 18, canto and alto).

70. See [1] "Mirate che m'ha fatto," mm. 20ff., [7] "Lo core mio," mm. 25ff., [5] "Gioia mia dolc' e cara," mm. 26ff., and [4] "Un' ape esser vorei," mm. 30–32, respectively. In "Un' ape esser vorei" the cadence on A at the word *inganni* (see mm. 31–32) is notated in the source with both a G-sharp and a B-flat in the penultimate harmony. If this is not a misprint, it forms a rather extraordinary parody of madrigalistic word painting!

71. There are two exceptions to this practice. See note 74 below.

72. See, for example, Don Harrán, "New Evidence for Musica Ficta: The Cautionary Sign," *Journal of the American Musicological Society* 29 (1976): 86. See also Rudolf von Ficker, "Beiträge zur Chromatik des 14. bis 16. Jahrhunderts," *Studien zur Musikwissenschaft* 2 (1914): 5–33.

73. James Haar, "False Relations and Chromaticism in Sixteenth-Century Music," *Journal of the American Musicological Society* 30 (1977): 391–418.

74. There are two exceptions to this practice. (1) In [7] "Io piansi un tempo," the a'-flat in m. 21, canto, cannot be held through m. 23 in view of the A-natural in the bass; the canto must thus rise chromatically either in m. 22 (as given here) or in m. 23. (2) A similar situation arises in [16] "È ben ragion," mm. 41–44. See the Critical Commentary for these works.

75. In rare instances, cadential ficta have been added at avoided cadences that do not contain the 6–8 or 3–1 in two voices, but are made strong by other means (e.g., the presence of a suspension and turn, or rests following the cadence in several voices).

76. This policy has also been followed for several strong internal cadences (e.g., Book 1, [18] "Donna, l'ardente fiamma," m. 35).

77. In the *Madrigali a 5* musical repetition sometimes begins in the middle of a text line. In these cases, the beginning of the repeated section is capitalized in this edition. In most cases, the beginnings of poetic lines are capitalized in the original source at all repetitions.

# Critical Commentary

The notes and comments below include citations of variants between the unique or principal source that have been corrected in the present edition, variant readings from supplementary sources, and discussions of passages that might be subject to more than a single interpretation. Errors or alterations in the poetic texts are cited in "Notes on the Text" in Texts and Translations. References are identified by title, measure number, and voice part (*C, A, Q, T, B* for canto, alto, quinto, tenore, and basso; *C1* for canto primo, etc.). Abbreviations for note values include: Br = breve, SB = semibreve, Mi = minim, SM = semiminim, and Fa = fusa. Pitch notation uses c′ for middle C and always reflects sounding pitch.

## Madrigali a 4 (1564)

### [1] *Non vide Febo mai*

Mm. 17 and 19, *T:* although the performer might wish to flat each e′ here, the editor suggests e′-naturals in order to preserve the motive in the same form as it appears in the *A,* m. 17 and the *B,* m. 18; ficta is not possible in the *A* and *B* as it would create diminished fifths with other voices.

### [2] *Stando per maraviglia*

M. 11, *T:* both e′s on beat 2 have sharps, presumably to warn the singer against flatting them by musica ficta rules at this point.   M. 36, *C:* sharps misplaced: first sharp appears before the e′; second sharp appears after the second f′.

*Ma 'l cor che stava*

M. 5, *A:* note 1 must be shortened to an eighth note because of the uninflected f in the *B*. While cross relations (particularly those involving a sharped note at the end of a phrase and an uninflected note at the beginning of the next one) are extremely frequent in the *Madrigali a 4,* only one direct overlap occurs in this collection. For further discussion, see the section on musica ficta under Editorial Procedures.

### [3] *Gratia non vider mai*

M. 31, *A:* notes 4 and 5 (g′ and f′) are Fas.

*Sì che non bramo*

M. 3, *A:* note 3 is not sharp; the stability of the harmony, the lack of a phrase division between the second and third f′, and the voice leading suggest that this omission is an error.   M. 13, *T:* dot after note 2 is missing.

### [4] *Qual gratia sparse mai*

M. 31, *A:* the cadence to G in m. 32 and the fact that the lower voices are sustained suggest that the absence of a sharp on note 3 is an error in the print.

*Se di bellezza il sol*

M. 10: the change in the *B* on the last note of the measure suggests that the absence of a sharp on note 6 in the *A* is an error; the solution proposed here coordinates the chromatic alteration with the harmony change, as is normal in Caimo's style.   M. 14, *C:* note 1 is a′; *B:* note 1 is f. The resulting dissonances are foreign to Caimo's style. The solution presented here is consistent with the types of progressions used in this work and others; cf. the voice leading in mm. 6, 9–10, 18–19, and 22.

### [6] *Chi vuol veder in terra*

*Ella coi rai*

The title of the *seconda parte* does not appear in the table of contents because both parts of this work are printed on the same page.

### [7] *Se potesse morir*

M. 17, *T:* the cadence on beat 3 and the lack of any movement in the other parts on beat 2 suggest that the absence of a sharp on note 2 is an error.   M. 23, *A:* sharp for note 3 placed on wrong line.

### [8] *Sestina: Che pro mi vien*

M. 17, *A:* note 3 is dotted.

*S'armata il cor*

Title in the table of contents reads, "S'armata il cor di."

*Scalda col tuo valore*

Mm. 15–16, *B:* explicit sharps occur only on notes 2 and 3 in m. 15; m. 15, note 1 and m. 16, note 1 cannot be altered because of the presence of perfect consonances in other voices. The situation here parallels that in m. 14.

*O desta in lei pietate*

M. 3, *T:* notes 3 and 4 are SMs.

*China le sant' orecchie*

M. 5, *A:* source shows a SM rest.

## [10] *Li vostr' occhi*

M. 19, *A:* note 1 is e'.   M. 28, *C:* note 3 is a SM.

## [11] *Anchor che col partire*

M. 5, *A:* source gives note 3 as c', but an f' has been written over this note by hand. Einstein (*Italian Madrigal,* 3:214–15) gives f', but this rendition creates parallel octaves with *B*. Mm. 9–10, *C:* Einstein (ibid.) shows m. 9, note 6 and m. 10, note 1 as two separate SMs; source shows a single Mi here.   Mm. 17 and 26, *C:* sharp on note 5 necessitated by written-in c'-sharp in *T* on last note of measure; alternatively, both voices could sing c-natural; Einstein (ibid.) shows c'-sharp in *T* simultaneously with c'-natural in *C*.   M. 18, *T:* Einstein (ibid.) shows note 2 as d'; source reads e'.   M. 31, *T:* note 4 is a dotted SB.

## [12] *E se tu, riva, udisti*

M. 6, *C:* sharp on note 3.   Mm. 14–20: that chromatic lines are intentional here is confirmed by octaves (e.g., in mm. 14, 18, and 19). See the discussion of this matter under Editorial Procedures.

## [13] *Andate, o miei sospiri*

Title in the table of contents reads, "Andate, o miei sospir ove."   Mm. 14–15 and 28, *B:* natural signs before every B.   M. 19, *T:* note 3 is d'.   M. 21, *C:* beat 1 is a Br rest with the lower half crossed out.   M. 24, *A:* natural signs precede every b' in this measure, apparently to warn the singer not to add b'-flat as indicated in m. 23.   M. 29, *A:* note 1 is a Mi. The sustained harmony in the lower three voices and the voice leading suggest that the absence of a sharp on note 2 is an error.

## [15] *Piangi, colle sacrato*

Source contains the following errors: M. 4, *T:* last note is a SB; m. 16, *A:* note 3 is c", but a ledger line appears above the note; m. 26, *A:* dot after note 2 is missing.

### *Lagrimate, voi fiumi*

M. 15, *T:* the short durations of notes 2 and 3 might suggest that the absence of a sharp on note 3 is an error. However, since a new phrase begins on note 3, the editor suggests that the publication is accurate and that no sharp was intended.   Mm. 16–19: source contains several radically dissonant harmonies, which appear to be errors primarily, but not exclusively, in the *T*. The editor, though hesitant about the number of changes, has nevertheless felt compelled to consider this passage erroneous and correct it in a manner consistent with Caimo's style. Unfortunately, no single explanation covers all of the errors. It is possible that the publisher copied from two different sources or that for mm. 16–17 he temporarily reversed the *T* and *A* parts. It is possible that at some point this passage was revised in a score format but that the revisions were incompletely transferred to the partbooks. The *A* and *T* parts may thus represent an intermediate compositional stage. Note that the harmonic progression in mm. 16–17 and 18–20 (A-major, D-minor, G-major, C-major, F-major, D-minor) also occurs in mm. 15–16, 21–22, and 27–28. The source shows the following apparent errors. M. 16, *A:* notes 4 and 5 are g's, last note is a SB; *T:* notes 3 and 4 are f'.   M. 17, *T:* note 1 is e'; *A:* note 1 is a Mi.   M. 18, *T:* note 3 is f'.   M. 19, *T:* notes 2–5 are e'.

## [16] *Piangete, valli*

Mm. 1–4: that the sharps were intended to apply only to one note is confirmed by the *B*, m. 3, beat 4, where d-natural is required by d' in the *A*; and by the *B*, m. 4, beat 2, where c-natural is required by an octave in the *T*. Einstein concurs in presenting a chromatic line in all voices. M. 8, *A:* note 3 is e'-flat, which is not possible with the e' in the *C*; the alternative reading, flatting the e' in the *C*, creates a horizontal tritone. While the intervening rest might make this interpretation possible, the reader should compare the beginning of "E se tu, riva, udisti," where the identical figure occurs in the *A* and *B* without the flat. For the relationship of these two pieces, see p. ix above.   Mm. 23 and 27, *A:* the naturals on m. 23, note 4 and m. 27, note 1 conform to the publisher's editorial policy in the *Madrigali a 4;* see "Musica Ficta" in the Preface. The chromatic alteration here is also parallel to that in the *C* in m. 24.   M. 28, *A:* on the prevalence of cross relations in the *Madrigali a 4,* see "Musica Ficta" in the Preface.

## [17] *Ardir, senno, virtù*

Title in the table of contents reads, "Ardir, ardir, se non virtù." M. 3, *C:* the parallel with mm. 9–10, where the same progression contains explicit accidentals, suggests that the absence of a sharp on note 5 is an error. This interpretation is further supported by the stability of the harmony and the voicing of the chord, along with its movement to a D-major triad on the next beat.

## [18] *Dialogo a 8 voci: Donna, l'ardente fiamma*

Title in table of contents reads only "Dialogo à 8. voci." M. 18, *C1:* sharp on note 4 is required by the explicit f-sharp in *A2*.   M. 19, *A2:* the short duration of note 2, the voice leading, and the lack of a phrase division between notes 1 and 2 suggest that the absence of a sharp on note 2 is an error.  M. 22, *A2:* the short durations of notes 4 and 5, the voice leading, and the lack of a phrase division between notes 4 and 5 suggest that the absence of a flat on note 5 is an error.  M. 35, *C1:* the sharp on note 4 supports the strong internal cadence; cf. mm. 4, 8, 10, et al., where a sharp is specified at phrase endings.

## Madrigali a 5 (1584/85)

### [2] *Come esser può*

M. 10, *A:* g'-natural is suggested on notes 2 and 3 because (1) the new phrase begins at this point, and (2) addition of this accidental allows the motive to match as closely as possible the same figure in the *T* in m. 7 (the change of harmony in the second presentation of this motive requires the f'-sharp in the *A* in m. 11 to avoid a tritone with the b in the *T*).  Mm. 39 and 64, *A:* note 1 must be sung as an eighth note, eighth rest; sharping the *Q*'s f' is highly questionable since the next note must be f'-natural in view of the f' in the *C*; see discussion of this passage under Editorial Procedures.

### [3] *Va lieto a mort' il core*

M. 4, *C:* sharp on note 4.

### [4] *Vedesti, Amor, giamai*

M. 27, *T:* note 4 is g.

### [5] *Gel' ha madonna il core*

M. 62, *A:* sharp on note 3 added by analogy with previous statements of this motive in mm. 55, 56, and 61.

### [6] *Thirsi morir volea*

M. 4, *A:* both notes 5 and 6 have sharps.  M. 13, *Q:* both notes 2 and 3 have sharps.  M. 18, *B:* rest 1 given as a Br rest.

#### *E mentre il guardo*

M. 18, *A:* note 7 is e'.  M. 31, *B:* note 7 is a SM.

### [7] *Io piansi un tempo*

Mm. 21–23, *C:* explicit a'-flat in m. 21 cannot be retained through all repetitions of this pitch in view of the A in the *B*, m. 23. The editor suggests raising the *C*'s a'-flat to a'-natural in m. 22, producing the third-related major triads typical of Caimo's style; an alternative is to change to a'-natural in m. 23; see Preface, note 74.  M. 24, *Q:* rest is a Br.  M. 25, *A:* sharps on both notes 1 and 2.  M. 34, *Q:* note 2 is a dotted SM; interpretation in this edition is consistent

with repetition of the phrase in m. 55; an alternative solution would be to retain the dot and halve the value of m. 34, note 3.  M. 64, *B:* rest missing.

### [8] *Parto da voi*

M. 57, *B:* sharp on note 2 added by analogy with m. 60.

### [9] *Mi suggean l'api il mele*

M. 13, *C:* flat on note 3 added by analogy with m. 15, *B*.

### [10] *Poi che 'l mio largo pianto*

M. 101, *B:* rest is a Br.

### [11] *Poi che ne' bei sospiri*

M. 7, *A:* sharps on both notes 1 and 2.  Mm. 37 and 62, *T:* sharp on note 1 added for cadence and because of explicit sharp in the *C*; although cross relations are frequent in Caimo's style, they always occur as a sharp followed by a natural at the beginning of the next phrase, never the reverse.

### [12] *Scoprirò l'ardor mio*

M. 31 and 36, *A:* m. 31, note 5 and m. 36, note 3 are natural here but sharped at the repetition of the phrase (mm. 46 and 51).  M. 37, *Q:* clef placed on wrong line for one staff only.  Mm. 38, 41, 53, and 56, *C:* see note under "Poi che ne' bei sospiri," mm. 37 and 62.  M. 57, *T:* note 3 is sharp in source; cf. m. 42.

#### *Risposta: Se voi sete il mio sol*

M. 40, *T:* note 1 is natural here, but sharp on repeat (m. 61).  M. 43, *B:* note 3 is g here but f on repeat (m. 64).  M. 53, *T:* sharps on both notes 1 and 2.

### [13] *Se voi set' il mio cor*

M. 33, *T:* note 1 is a' here but g' on repeat (m. 52).  Mm. 38 and 57, *A*, mm. 44 and 63, *Q:* variant in rhythm appears here as given in source.

### [14] *Che fa hoggi il mio sole*

M. 25, *A:* sharp on note 1 added by analogy with similar statement at m. 17.  M. 36, *Q:* note 1 is natural here, but flatted at the repetition of the phrase in m. 54.  M. 65, *T:* extra Mi rest.

### [15] *Chi mov' il piè*

M. 13, *C:* sharps on both notes 1 and 2.  M. 21, *Q:* extra Br rest.  M. 38, *Q:* natural on final c' mandated by m. 39, *C*, note 1 (c").  Mm. 42–43, *T:* sharp placed in front of m. 43, note 1 rather than m. 42, note 3.

## [16] *È ben ragion*

M. 19, *Q:* sharps on both notes 1 and 2.  M. 43, *A:* explicit d'-flat in m. 41 cannot be retained through all repetitions of this pitch in view of the G's in the *B* and *C* in m. 44. The suggestion to raise the pitch to d'-natural in m. 43 creates third-related major triads and coordinates the chromatic alteration with the change in bass, both of which are typical of Caimo's style; an alternative is to change to d'-natural in m. 44.  M. 48, *B:* extra SB rest.  M. 51, *A:* sharps on both notes 3 and 4.  M. 60, *C:* f-natural might be possible at note 2 in view of the text and by analogy with the harmony of m. 54.  M. 74, *A:* sharps on both notes 1 and 2; *Q:* note 2 is sharp.

## [17] *Canzone: O sola, o senza par*

M. 31, *A:* sharp on note 2 added by analogy with m. 29, *B.*  M. 36, *A:* rest is a SM.

### *Amor vid' io*

Title in the table of contents reads, "Amor vid' io che del."

### *Come in arido legno*

M. 7, *Q:* note 2 is d.  Mm. 30–31, *C:* text reads "se stesso oblia."  M. 56, *Q:* note 3 is a SM.

## *From* **Fiamma ardente a 5 (1586)**

### [1] *Mirate che m'ha fatto*

M. 6, *C:* note 1 is a SM.  M. 22, *C:* clef placed on wrong line here.

### [2] *Date la vela al vento*

M. 14, *C:* notes 2 and 3 are Fas.  M. 18, *C,* notes 4 and 5 are Fas.  M. 26, *Q:* sharp on note 1.

### [3] *Bene mio, tu m'hai lasciato*

Title in the table of contents reads, "Bene mio tu m'hai."  Mm. 8–9, *C:* text setting in the present edition follows that in *Nervi d'Orfeo.*  M. 12, *A:* repetition of word *alcun* occurs only in *Paradiso musicale* and *Nervi d'Orfeo.*  M. 18, *A:* sharps on notes 3–5 (all g's).  Mm. 23 and 38, *A:* sharps on both notes 1 and 2. Performers should resist the temptation to make note 2 natural in order to conform to the repetition of the phrase at the end of the measure. The f'-sharp for the first statement of *morirò* is explicit both times, whereas the repetition must use f'-natural in view of the F's and the C in the other parts.  Mm. 32 and 47, *A:* the word *deh* appears in *Paradiso musicale* only.  Mm. 41–43, *A:* sharps suggested by analogy with mm. 26–27, where they are explicit.

### [4] *Un' ape esser vorei*

M. 11, *T:* clef on wrong line for one staff only.  M. 31, *C:* sharp on note 4—impossible in view of the *T*'s

b-flat. Alternatively, the *T* could sing b-natural. It is possible that the presence of both accidentals represents a naive portrayal of *inganni.* See discussion in the Preface, note 70.

## [5] *Gioia mia dolc' e cara*

Title in the table of contents reads, "Gioia mia dolce."  M. 9, *Q:* note 1 is c'; changed by analogy with m. 9, *C;* mm. 9–10 and m. 13, *T;* and m. 12, *Q.*  M. 16, *A:* sharp on note 3.  Mm. 35 and 47, *C:* note 1 should possibly be a'; however, the source shows b' in both instances.

## [6] *Dolci sospir'*

M. 27, *T:* note 2 is a here but is g at the repetition in m. 37.  M. 35, *C:* natural on note 1 suggested by analogy with m. 25, where it is explicit.  Mm. 39–40, *A:* the g' is a Mi, rather than a SB.

## [7] *Lo core mio*

M. 14, *Q:* notes 5 and 6 are SMs.  Mm. 16–17, *T:* text reads "martell' e Tic e toc."  M. 20, *C:* note 2 is c"; cf. mm. 18–19, *B.*

## [8] *Vola, vola, pensier*

M. 4, *A:* note 1 is b'-flat, but c" at the repetition in m. 11.  M. 8, *C:* flat on note 1 is suggested by analogy with m. 1.  M. 34, *C:* explicit natural on note 2 is clearly cautionary, preventing the singer from adding the e"-flat suggested by the melodic line; the cautionary *mi* here avoids a diminished fifth with the *A* and *B.*

## [10] *Canzone: Partomi, donna*

M. 3, *Q:* sharps on notes 1 and 2.  M. 5, *T:* note 2 is a'.  Mm. 10–12: repetition of "e teco lascio il core" in place of "per pegno de mia constant'e forte" in the *C* only.  Mm. 27 and 40, *T:* sharp on note 3 suggested in view of C-sharps in mm. 27–28, and mm. 40–41, *C* and *A;* note 3 could possibly be sung as c'-natural; if so, the *C* must shorten c"-sharp to an eighth note.

### *Forz' è ch'io parti*

M. 3, *A:* note 1 is b', but c" at the repetition in m. 21.  M. 11, *B:* text reads "dolce mio"; all other parts read "mio dolce."  M. 16, *C:* sharp on note 1 suggested by analogy with m. 34, where it is explicit.  M. 27, *B:* note 1 is a SM, but a Mi at the prior statement in m. 9.  M. 52, *T:* note 3 is a SB, but a Mi at the prior statement in m. 45, *Q.*

### *Haimè, meschino*

M. 17, *T:* note 2 is a; changed by analogy with m. 36, *Q.*  M. 18, *A:* note 2 is a Mi; changed by analogy with m. 37.  M. 26, *Q:* note 2 is a Mi; changed by analogy with m. 7, *T*.   M. 38, *T:* natural on note 3 is mandated by the octave in the *C;* the absence of this indication is obviously an error.   M. 42, *Q:* note 3 is a SM, but a Mi at the repetition in mm. 49–50, *T.*

## [11] *Occhi leggiadri*

Mm. 6–10, *T:* text phrases are reversed in source; changed by analogy with mm. 20–24.

## [12] *Questa crudel*

M. 18, *Q:* dot missing on note 1.   M. 35, *T:* sharp on note 4 added by analogy with m. 29, where it is explicit.   M. 46, *B:* rest omitted.   M. 47, *A:* sharp on note 2; changed to avoid an augmented sixth with the *Q.*

## [13] *'Na volta m'hai gabbato*

M. 2, *T:* note 2 is a.   M. 18, *T:* note 1 is a.   M. 21, *A:* note 3 is a SM.   Mm. 29–30, *B:* source reads d (SB), G (Mi), Mi rest. The error may have occurred during the transference to partbooks; note that at the repetition of this passage (mm. 37–38) rhythmic values are augmented.

## [14] *Con tue lusinghe, Amore*

Mm. 37 and 55, *A:* source supports variant rhythm at repeat, as given here.   Mm. 47 and 65, *Q:* natural on note 2 suggested by analogy with mm. 43 and 61.

# Texts and Translations

## Translations by Robert Durling

Critical notes below specify variants between the text in this edition and that in the original music prints and clarify obscure passages in the poetry. In all cases, spellings in this section correspond to those in the music. The orthographic policy used in this edition is detailed under Editorial Procedures. The word *source* in the notes below refers to the musical print used as the basis for these transcriptions. Also specified beneath the texts are the poetic sources consulted for this edition, either authoritative modern editions or the original poetic collection.

## Book 1, Madrigali a 4 (1564)

### [1] *Non vide Febo mai*

| | |
|---|---|
| Non vide Febo mai da l'Indo al Mauro, | Phoebus never saw, from the Indus to the Maurus, |
| Più nobil coppia, o più verace essempio | A more noble couple or a truer example |
| Di vertù, di bellezza, onde restauro | Of virtue, of beauty, by which |
| Stanca natura prende nel suo tempio. | Weary nature finds restoration in her temple. |
| Mirando la degn' opra e 'l bel thesauro, | Looking at their worthy works and beautiful treasure, |
| Invidia pugne Amor lascivo et empio, | Envy pierces lustful and cruel Love, |
| Ma Ludovico a sè suave il piega, | But Ludovico bends him sweetly to himself |
| E Portia col bel crin lo stringe e lega. | And Portia ties and binds him with her beautiful hair. |

NOTE ON THE TEXT: Dedicatory madrigal for Ludovico Galerato.

### [2] *Stando per maraviglia*

*[Prima parte]*

| | |
|---|---|
| Stando per maraviglia [a] mirar fiso | As I stood in wonder looking fixedly |
| Quel sol che mi consuma in fiamma e 'n gelo, | At that sun which consumes me in fire and frost, |
| Ratto un tuon folgorando uscio dal cielo, | Suddenly lightning and thunder came forth from heaven |
| Per farmi privo ond' era sì diviso. | To deprive me of what was so separated from me. |
| Qual nuova invidia è nata in paradiso, | What strange envy has been born in paradise, |
| Acciò che innanz' il tempo io cang' il pelo? | To make my hair turn white before its time? |
| Hor non basta la guerra del bel velo, | Is not the barrier of the beautiful veil, which |
| Che sì spesso mi vieta gli occhi e 'l viso? | So often forbids me to see her eyes and face, enough? |

*Seconda parte*

| | |
|---|---|
| Ma 'l cor che stava desioso e 'ntento | But my heart, which was desirously intent |
| Ai dolci raggi de bei lumi honesti, | On the sweet rays of her lovely virtuous eyes, |
| Poco curava i tuon, la pioggia e 'l vento; | Cared little for the thunder, rain, and wind; |
| E fra tanti terrori atri e funesti | And among so many black and ominous terrors |
| Seco dicea per duol non per spavento: | Said to itself, in grief not in fear: |
| Tant' ire son negli animi celesti? | Is there such anger in the spirits of heaven? |

AUTHOR: Jacopo Sannazaro
POETIC SOURCE: Jacopo Sannazaro, *Opere volgari*, ed. Alfredo Mauro (Bari: Gius. Laterza & Figli, 1961), 194 ("Sonetti e canzoni," no. 77).
NOTE ON THE TEXT: *Prima parte*, line 2, source reads *consumma* for *consuma*.

## [3] *Gratia non vider mai*

*[Prima parte]*

Gratia non vider mai huomin' o Dei  
Più gratiosa o vaga o più gentile  
Di quella che già i' vidi così humile,  
Ingombrata d'honor e di trophei:  
L'alme virtù che risplendon in lei  
Le bellezze immortal co 'l degno stile,  
Gl'altier costumi che da Battro a Tile  
Risuonan, m'han supposto alli su'omei.

Men and gods never saw a Grace  
More gracious, more beautiful, or more noble  
Than her whom I saw once humble,  
Now laden with honors and trophies.  
The noble virtues that shine in her,  
The immortal beauties and worthy style,  
The noble ways whose fame resounds  
As far as Bactria and Thule, have made me her slave.

*Seconda parte*

Sì che non bramo, non voglio, in cielo, in terra,

Altro che gratia di mia vita, speme,  
E del mio cor refugio e sol contento,  
Però non sia donn' altra che m'afferra  
Con sua bellezza il cuor e l'alma insieme,  
Che pria vorrò esser di vita spento.

So that I do not desire, I do not wish, in heaven or on earth,  
Anything but grace from her who is my life, my hope,  
The refuge and sole happiness of my heart,  
Therefore let there never be another lady to seize  
With her beauty my heart and soul together,  
For I shall rather wish my life to be extinguished.

NOTE ON THE TEXT: *Prima parte,* line 3, source reads *vide* for *vidi.*

## [4] *Qual gratia sparse mai*

*[Prima parte]*

Qual gratia sparse mai l'eterno Giove  
Qua giù fra noi, suoi miseri mortali,  
Maggior di questa in cui il fanciul dall' ali  
S'annid' e in copia le sue gratie piove?  
Oh rara gratia che di gratie nuove  
Mi riemp' il cuor, ma con pungenti strali!  
Odi Eccho risuonar tutte le vali:  
"Gratia e beltà d'ogn' uno muove."

What grace did eternal Jove ever scatter  
Down here among us, his wretched mortals,  
Greater than this [Grace] in whom the winged boy  
Has his nest and plentifully pours out his graces?  
Oh rare Grace who fills my heart  
With new graces but with piercing arrows!  
You hear Echo resounding in all the valleys,  
"She takes grace and beauty away from all others."

*Seconda parte*

Se di bellezza il sol, di Gratia Giuno

Avanzi, e Palas d'eloquenza passi,  
Come farai ch'in te Gratia non trovi?

Se sei scesa dal ciel e da quell' uno  
E trino Giove ornata, haimè, non lassi  
Adietro ogn' altra, deh pietà ti muovi.

If you surpass the beauty of the sun, the Grace of Juno,  
And the eloquence of Pallas [Athena],  
How will you bring it about that I not find Grace in you?  
If you are descended from the sky and  
Adorned by the one and triple Jove, alas, do not leave  
Me behind for another; move yourself in pity.

NOTES ON THE TEXT: *Prima parte,* line 3, "il fanciul dall' ali" ("the winged boy") is, of course, Cupid; line 4, source reads *coppia* for *copia;* line 8, source reads *gratia* for *Gratia. Seconda parte,* lines 4–5, "quell' uno e trino Giove" ("the one and triple Jove") mixes references to the Trinity with pagan mythology; line 6, source reads *dhe* for *deh.*

## [5] *Eccelsa e generosa prole*

*[Prima parte]*

Eccelsa e generosa prole degna  
E di Re Patre e d'Avo Imperatore

Lofty and generous progeny, worthy  
Of your father, the King, and your grandfather, the Emperor

| | |
|---|---|
| De' quai la gloria, e 'l sopr' human valore | Whose glory and superhuman valor |
| Qual' habbiate a seguir sentier v'insegna, | Show you the path you should follow, |
| Siavi ad ogn' hor più amica e più benigna | Let each star in heaven be ever more friendly and kind |
| | |
| Ogni stella del ciel co 'l cui favore | To you, with whose favor |
| Lieti nel sen v'accolga, anzi nel core, | Let your noble uncle, who reigns in Spain, gladly |
| L'alto zio vostro ch'in Ispagna regna. | Welcome you to his bosom, even to his heart. |

*Seconda parte*

| | |
|---|---|
| Sotto l'ombra del qual sì cresce in voi | Under his shadow, virtue so grows in you |
| Con gl'anni la virtù che stupor dia | With the years that it will amaze |
| Al secol da venir non ch'al presente. | The age to come as well as the present one. |
| Giunti a l'età del vestir l'armi poi | When you have finally reached the age of bearing arms, |
| La forz' e 'l senno tal, tal l'ardir sia | Let your force, your wisdom, and your daring be such |
| Ch'inalzi Europa e faccia Asia dolente. | That they may raise up Europe and make Asia mourn. |

NOTE ON THE TEXT: Dedicatory sonnet for the sons of Maximilian II.

## [6] *Chi vuol veder in terra*

[*Prima parte*]

| | |
|---|---|
| Chi vuol veder in terra, | Whoever wishes to see on earth |
| Quanto di bel fe' la natura e Dio | As much beauty as nature and God ever made, |
| Miri costei ch'[è] un sol al parer mio. | Let him gaze on her, who is a sun, it seems to me. |

*Seconda parte*

| | |
|---|---|
| Ella coi rai atterra | With her rays she casts to earth |
| Ogni vista mortal come far suole | Every mortal eye, as does |
| Gratia che vien' innanzi al nuovo sole | The Grace who precedes the rising sun; |
| E poi al dolce riso | And then at her sweet smile |
| Ride la terra, s'apre 'l paradiso. | The earth smiles and heaven opens. |

NOTE ON THE TEXT: *Seconda parte,* line 1, source reads *con* for *coi.*

## [7] *Se potesse morir*

| | |
|---|---|
| Se potesse morir meco il desio, | If my desire could die with me, |
| Ch'è sì possente e forte, | My desire so powerful and strong, |
| Io bramarei la morte | I would yearn for death |
| Per far meco mortal il desir mio. | So as to make it mortal with me. |
| Ma sì vivace [in cor vive il desire,] | But so alive in my heart is my desire, |
| [Ch'amar] mi fa vostra bellezza tanto | It makes me love your beauty so much |
| Che per dolor, per pianto, | That in spite of sorrow, in spite of weeping, |
| Nè per lieto gioire, | In spite of ravishing joy itself, |
| Fra mille mort' io non potrei morire. | Amid a thousand deaths I could not die. |

AUTHOR: Luigi Cassola

POETIC SOURCE: Luigi Cassola, *Madrigali* (Venice: Gabriel Giolito de Ferrar', 1544), 32 (no. 141).

NOTES ON THE TEXT: Line 1, source reads *mirar* for *morir*; lines 5–6, words in brackets appear in poetic collection but are omitted in the musical setting; English translation of the text without the bracketed words: ''But your beauty makes me so full of life.''

## [8] *Sestina: Che pro mi vien*

*[Prima parte]*

Che pro mi vien ch'io t'abbia, o bella diva

  Che reggi 'l terzo cielo,
Su questa verd' e dilettosa riva
Sacrato un mirto il cui frondoso crine
Non teme ira di ghiacci' o di pruine?

What profit comes to me from having, O lovely
    goddess
Who rules the third heaven,
On this green and pleasant shore
Consecrated to you a myrtle, whose leafy locks
Fear not the wrath of ice or frost,

*Seconda parte*

S'armata il cor di mattutino gelo
  Sprezz' il tuo dolce foco
La vezzosa Terilla e dal suo stelo
Troncò la speme all' hor che 'l vago fiore
Apria le foglie e si mostrava fuore.

If, her heart armed with morning frost,
Charming Terilla scorns
Your sweet fire and from its stem
Has cut my hope just when its lovely flower
Was opening its petals and letting itself be seen?

*Terza parte*

Scalda col tuo valore a poco a poco
  I suoi pensier gelati;
Scema l'orgoglio sì che trovi loco,
Dove s'appoggi ne la fredda mente
Il mio desir via più d'ogn' altro ardente.

With your power, warm little by little
Her frozen thoughts;
Lessen her pride, so that my desire,
Much more ardent than any other's,
May find a place to rest in her cold mind.

*Quarta parte*

Non consentir come negl' anni andati
  Ch'io facci' ardent' e molli
Quest' aria di sospir, di pianto i prati
Et che del fero mio stat' infelice
Risuoni anchor Italia d'ogni pendice.

Do not consent, as in past years,
That I heat this air
With sighs, moisten the field with tears,
And that every cliff in Italy still
Resound with my cruel unhappy state.

*Quinta parte*

O desta in lei pietate, o i desir folli
  Humor di dolce oblio
Spenga in me sì che queste piagg' et colli
Parlin meco di gioia e di diletto,
Et di mesti pensier sia sgombro il petto.

Either awaken pity in her, or let my mad desires
A sweet dew of forgetfulness
Extinguish in me, so that these slopes and hills
May speak with me of joy and delight
And my breast be freed of its sad cares.

*Sesta parte*

China le sant' orecchie al canto mio,
  Nè ti mostrar più schiva,
O regina di Cipro, al bel desio,
Ch'ogn' anno havrai ne la nova stagione
Di vagh' et lieti fior mille corone.

Incline your holy ears to my song,
No longer be unfavorable,
O queen of Cyprus, to my sweet desire,
And every year in springtime you shall have
A thousand garlands made of lovely flowers.

AUTHOR: Bernardo Tasso
POETIC SOURCE: *Rime di M. Bernardo Tasso*, vol. 2 (Bergamo: Pietro Lancellotti, 1749), 216–17 (Ode 14).
NOTES ON THE TEXT: *Prima parte*, line 2, " il terzo cielo" ("the third heaven") is the heaven of Venus according to Ptolemaic cosmology. *Quarta parte*, line 2, source reads *faci'* for *facci'*. *Quinta parte*, line 1, source reads *destra* for *desta*; table of contents reads *pietade*, but all parts read *pietate*; line 2, source reads *dolc' oblio* for *dolce oblio*. *Sesta parte*, line 4, lower three parts read *nova*, canto reads *nostra*; Tasso poetic collection reads *nova*.

## [9] *I capegli d'or fin*

I capegli d'or fin, di neve il viso,
E 'l gentil volto candido e rosato,

Her hair of fine gold, her countenance of snow,
And her noble face, white and rosy,

Quei vaghi lumi sciolt' in paradiso
Per dar al sol qua giù soccorso grato,
L'angelico soave e dolce riso
Ch'esce di perle e di coralli ornato,
Fan una Margarita sì pretiosa
Ch'ogni gemma al suo par venir non osa.

Those lovely lights that opened in paradise
To give to the sun down here a welcome help,
Her angelic, sweet, and gentle laugh
That comes out embellished with pearls and coral—
All go to make a Pearl so precious
That no gem dares to be compared with her.

## [10] *Li vostr' occhi*

Li vostr' occhi che sembran due facelle
Un giorno vidi che credei morire;
Certo credei che fossero due stelle.
Rendete il cor e fatemi gioire
E non mi fate star più, o viso bello,
Tant' adirato che non possa udire
I vostri canti che son sì soavi
Al par dei bei vostr' occhi così gravi

Your eyes, which seem two torches,
I saw one day and I believed I would die;
Certainly I believed them to be two stars.
Surrender your heart and give me joy,
And do not make me wait any longer, O lovely face,
In such sadness that I cannot hear
Your songs, which are as sweet
As your beautiful solemn eyes.

## [11] *Anchor che col partire*

Anchor che col partire
  Io mi sento morire,
Partir vorrei ogn' hor, ogni momento,
  Tant' [è] il piacer ch'io sento
De la vita ch'aquisto nel ritorno.
E così mill' e mille volt' il giorno
  Partir da voi vorrei
Tanto son dolci gli ritorni miei.

Although in parting
  I feel myself dying,
I would wish to part every hour, every moment,
So great is the pleasure I feel
In the life I acquire when I return.
And thus a thousand and a thousand times a day
  I would wish to leave you,
So sweet are my returnings to you.

AUTHOR: Alfonso d'Avalos
NOTE ON THE TEXT: For information about this text, see Ernest T. Ferand, "Anchor che col partire: Die Schicksale
  eines berühmten Madrigals," in *Festschrift Karl Gustav Fellerer* (Regensburg: Gustav Bosse, 1962), 137ff.

## [12] *E se tu, riva, udisti*

E se tu, riva, udisti alcuna volta
Humani affetti, hor prego, oh accompagni
La dolente sampogna a pianger volta!
O herbe, o fior, ch'un tempo eccelsi e magni
Re fosti al mondo, et hor per aspra sorte
Giacete per li fiumi e per li stagni,
[Venite tutti meco a pregar Morte,
Che, se esser può, finisca le mie doglie,
E gli rincresca il mio gridar sì forte.]

And if you, O shore, sometimes have listened
To human feelings, now, I pray you, accompany
My mournful bagpipe, which has turned to weeping!
O grass, O flowers, who once were exalted and great
Kings in the world, and now through bitter fate
Lie among the rivers and the marshes,
[Come, all of you, with me to pray to Death
That, if possible, she end my sorrows
And take pity on my loud crying.]

AUTHOR: Jacopo Sannazaro
POETIC SOURCE: "Arcadia," in Jacopo Sannazaro, *Opere volgari*, ed. Alfredo Mauro (Bari: Gius. Laterza & Figli,
  1961), 106 (Eclogue 11, lines 22–27).
NOTE ON THE TEXT: The three lines in brackets do not appear in Caimo's setting, but are taken from Sannazaro's
  text to complete the sentence. The text of this madrigal follows that of no. 16, "Piangete, valli," in Sannazaro's *Arcadia*. See Preface, p. ix.

## [13] *Andate, o miei sospiri*

Andate, o miei sospiri, ove abelisce
Con horribil chiome il capo de colubri,
O l'Hidra col sofiar ch'incrudelisce,
E 'l faro de Pluton co suoi delubri.

Go, my sighs, where [Medusa] adorns her head
With horrid locks of vipers,
Or where the Hydra with its cruel breath
And Pluto's beacon with his temple [reside].

Aimè, Caron già sento che languisce
D'haverm' in grembo nei Stigi lugubri,
Ma credo c'haverò tanta aqua ai lumi,
Malgrado d'Atropòs, che farò i fiumi.

Alas, I sense that Charon already yearns
To take me to his bosom by the mournful Styx,
But I believe I will have so much water in my eyes,
That, in spite of Atropos, I will create rivers.

NOTES ON THE TEXT: Line 1, source alternates between *sospiri* and *sospir* in text repetitions; line 3, source reads *incredulisce* for *incrudelisce;* line 4, source reads *to* for *co.*

## [14] *Gratia, voi sete*

Gratia, voi sete sì gioiosa e chiara,
Via più ch'il Sol e qual Fenice al mondo,
E chiaro il nome a cui il viso giocondo

Uguale che per tutt' orna e rischiara.
In voi tanta beltade altiera e rara
Chiaramente si vede a tond' a tondo
Ch'appò voi sola ogn' altra bella è al fondo,
Gratia d'ogni virtude al mondo chiara.

Grace, you are so joyous and bright,
More even than the Sun, like a Phoenix in the world,
And bright is your name, the equal of your happy
    face,
Which adorns and brightens everywhere.
In you, so much proud and rare beauty
One sees clearly, in its entirety,
That near you alone, all other beauties are eclipsed,
Grace bright with every virtue in the world.

## [15] *Piangi, colle sacrato*

*[Prima parte]*

Piangi, colle sacrat' opaco e fosco,
Et voi cave spelonch' e grotte oscure
Ululando venite a pianger nosco.
Piangete fagi e quercie alpestr' e dure,
E piangendo, narrate a questi sassi
Le nostre lagrimose aspre venture.

Weep, sacred hills, cloudy and dark,
And you caves, dens and shadowy grottos,
Howling, come weep with us.
Weep, beeches and hard alpine oaks,
And weeping, tell these rocks
Our tearful harsh misfortune.

*Seconda parte*

Lagrimate, voi fiumi ignudi e cassi
D'ogni dolcezza, e voi, fontane e rivi,
Fermate il corso, e retenete i passi.
E tu che fra le selve occulta vivi,
Echo mesta, rispondi a le parole
E quant' io parlo per li tronchi scrivi.

Shed tears, you rivers, bare and deprived
Of any sweetness, and you, fountains and streams,
Halt in your course and check your steps.
And you who live hidden within the woods,
Sad echo, respond to my words
And write what I speak upon the tree trunks.

AUTHOR: Jacopo Sannazaro
POETIC SOURCE: "Arcadia," in Jacopo Sannazaro, *Opere volgari,* ed. Alfredo Mauro (Bari: Gius. Laterza & Figli, 1961), 106 (Eclogue 11, lines 4–15).
NOTES ON THE TEXT: *Prima parte,* line 1, source reads *opacco* for *opaco. Seconda parte,* line 5, source reads *eccho* for *echo.*

## [16] *Piangete, valli*

Piangete, valli abbandonate e sole,
E tu, terra, dipingi nel tuo manto
I gigli oscuri e nere le viole.
La dotta Egeria e la Thebana Manto
Con subito furor morte n'ha tolta.
Ricominciate, o Muse, il vostro pianto.

Weep, you abandoned, lonely valleys,
And you, O earth, paint on your mantle
The darkened lilies and the violets turned black.
The learned Egeria and the Theban Manto
With sudden rage death has taken from us.
Begin again, O Muses, your lamenting.

AUTHOR: Jacopo Sannazaro
POETIC SOURCE: "Arcadia," in Jacopo Sannazaro, *Opere volgari,* ed. Alfredo Mauro (Bari: Gius. Laterza & Figli, 1961), 106 (Eclogue 11, lines 16–21).

## [17] *Ardir, senno, virtù*

Ardir, senno, virtù, bellezza e fede,
La fam' in terra com' immortal Dea,
Qual Dio non mosse prest' il santo piede
Quando conobbe del vermo l'Idea?
Giunon in lei con la ricchezza siede
Minerva saggia insieme e Citerea.
Qual huom selvaggio Ippolita non prezza
O vide'n donna mai più gran vaghezza?

Boldness, wisdom, beauty, and faith,
Fame on earth, like an immortal Goddess—
What God would not quickly move his holy foot
When he knew the Idea of the worm?
Juno with wealth resides in her [and]
Wise Minerva, as well as Cytherea.
What man is so savage that he does not prize Ippolita,
Or ever saw in a lady greater beauty?

NOTES ON THE TEXT: Line 1, source reads *Ardir se non virtù;* change of *se non* to *senno* is based on a text set by Rore, which uses the same initial line (see Rore's "Scielgan l'alme sorelle—Ardir, senno, virtù" [1544]); although Rore's first line is identical to Caimo's (with the exception of *senno* in place of *se non*), the remainder of the poem is different; however, *senno* more clearly fits the context of Caimo's as well as Rore's stanza. Lines 3–4, the Italian of these two lines is obscure; "del vermo l'Idea" ("the Idea of the worm") may refer to the Dal Verme family; Caimo's canzonette of 1584 are dedicated to Marcantonio Dal Verme (see Preface, note 28, for details). Line 6, "Citerea" ("Cytherea") is Venus; source reads *insieme è* for *insieme e*. Line 7, "Ippolita" is possibly the grandmother of Marcantonio Dal Verme (see Preface, note 28).

## [18] *Dialogo a 8 voci: Donna, l'ardente fiamma*

Donna, l'ardente fiamma
E la pena e 'l tormento
Cresc' in me tanto che morir mi sento.
  Deh vengavi desire
Di terminar' un giorno il mio martire
E di smorzar quel mio vivace ardore
Ch'io sarò vostro servo, e voi d'amore.

Lady, the ardent flame
And the suffering and torment
Grow in me so much that I am dying.
Ah, may you conceive the desire
Of one day ending my suffering
And extinguishing this my lively flame,
For I will be your servant, and you Love's.

Signor, la vostra fiamma
E la pena e 'l tormento
Non è ponto maggior di quel ch'io sento,
  Nè più grand' il desire
Di terminar il vostr' e 'l mio martire.
Ma se gl'avien ch'io smorz' il vostr' ardore,
Me privarò d'amante, e voi d'amore.

Sir, your flame
And suffering and torment
Is no greater than what I feel,
Nor is your desire greater [than mine]
To end your suffering and mine.
But if it happens that I extinguish your flame,
I deprive myself of a lover, you of love.

## Book 4, Madrigali a 5 (1584/85)

### [1] *Sculpio ne l'alma Amore*

  Sculpio ne l'alma Amore
L'immagin vostra e con sì ardente face
  L'abbruggia ogn' hor, che more,
Anzi ogni indugio di morir gli spiace,
E mentr' ella si pasce del desir
Di morte, [a morte] si fur' ella et io.

Love has carved your image in my soul,
And with so burning a torch
He keeps inflaming it, that it dies,
Or rather, finds all delay of death displeasing,
And while she feeds on the desire
For death, she steals herself from death, as do I.

NOTE ON THE TEXT: Line 6, the two words in brackets do not appear in Caimo's text, but are present in Casulana's setting of the same poem (see Preface, pages ix–x).

### [2] *Come esser può*

  Come esser può che 'l core
More, se mentre di morir gli piace
  E vago d'esser fuor
Del duol, più torn' in vita, e qual hor giace

How can my heart
Die, if when it delights to die
And yearns to leave
Its grief, it takes on more life, and when it lies

Più sepolto nel mal, cresce il desio
Di morte, et egli in lui s'aviv' et io.

Buried most in woe, its desire for death
Most grows, and in this desire it revives, as do I.

NOTE ON THE TEXT: Line 2, source reads *spiace* for *piace*.

## [3] *Va lieto a mort' il core*

Va lieto a mort' il core
Se sottrarsi morend' al duol gli piace,
 Ma'l piacer d'esser fuor
Di vita, in vita il tiene, e morto giace
Ond' è viv' egli sol del gran desio;
Di mort' e' morto viv' e tal anch' io.

Happy goes my heart to death,
If it rejoices to withdraw in death from grief;
But the joy of leaving
Life, keeps it in life though it lies dead,
And thus it lives on desire alone;
On death it dying lives, as do I.

NOTE ON THE TEXT: Line 2, source reads *spiace* for *piace*.

## [4] *Vedesti, Amor, giamai*

Vedesti, Amor, giamai di sì bel sole,

Sì belle luci, e di sì bella pietra
Uscir sì belle fiamme e 'n quell' un core,

Arder sì lieto e radopiar il foco,
Sì dolcemente radopiar il pianto,
E far d'i danni suoi pietoso il cielo?

Love, have you ever seen come forth from such a
 lovely sun
Such lovely lights, and from so lovely a stone
Such lovely flames, and [have you ever seen] in them
 a heart
Burn so gladly and redouble the fire,
So sweetly redouble the weeping,
And make heaven take pity on its grief?

## [5] *Gel' ha madonna il core*

Gel' ha madonna il core e fiamma il volto;
 Io son ghiaccio di fuore,
 Il foco è dentr' accolto.
 Questo vien perch' Amore
Ne la sua fronte alberga e nel mio petto,
 Nè mai cangia diletto
Si ch'io l'habbia ne gli occhi, ella nel core.

My lady has ice for a heart, flame for a face;
I am ice without,
The fire is all gathered within.
This comes about because Love
Dwells in her forehead and in my breast,
Nor does his pleasure ever change
So that I might have it before my eyes, she in her
 heart.

AUTHOR: Torquato Tasso
POETIC SOURCE: Angelo Solerti, ed., *Le Rime di Torquato Tasso*, vol. 2 (Bologna: Romagnoli-Dall' Acqua, 1898),
 381 ("Rime amorose estravaganti," no. 129).
NOTE ON THE TEXT: Line 1, Tasso's original text reads *seno* for *core*.

## [6] *Thirsi morir volea*

[*Prima parte*]

Thirsi morir volea
Gli occhi mirando di colei ch'adora,
Ond' ella che di lui non meno ardea,
 Gli disse, "Ohimè, ben mio,
 Deh non morir anchora,
Che teco bramo di morir anch' io."
 Frenò Thirsi il desio
C'havea di più sua vita alhor finire
E sentì morte e non potea morire.

Thyrsis wished to die,
Gazing into the eyes of the one he loves,
So she, who burned no less than he,
Said to him, "Alas, my love,
Ah, do not die yet,
For I too wish to die with you."
Thyrsis reined in his desire
To end his life at that moment,
And felt the pangs of death at not dying.

*Seconda parte*

E mentre il guardo fisso pur tenea
 Da i begli occhi divini
E nettar amoroso indi bevea,

And while he still fixed his gaze
On her beautiful divine eyes,
Still drinking thence Love's nectar,

| | |
|---|---|
| La bella Ninfa sua che già vicini | His lovely nymph, feeling |
|   Sentia i messi d'Amore | The messengers of Love draw near, |
| Disse con occhi languidi e tremanti, | Said with eyes languishing and trembling, |
|   "Mori, cor mio, ch'io moro." | "Die, my heart, for I am dying." |
| ["Ed io," rispose subito il pastore | ["And I," the shepherd answered quickly, |
| "E teco nel morir mi discoloro."] | "dying, grow pale along with you."] |
| Così morirno i fortunati amanti | So the fortunate lovers died |
| Di morte sì soave e sì gradita | A death so sweet and so welcome, |
| Che per anco morir tornar' in vita. | That in order to die again, they came back to life. |

AUTHOR: Battista Guarini

POETIC SOURCE: Luigi Fassò, ed., *Opere di Battista Guarini* (Torino: Unione Tipografica, 1950), 462 ("Concorso di occhi amorosi").

NOTES ON THE TEXT: *Prima parte,* line 2, source reads *ch'adoro* for *ch'adora. Seconda parte,* line 3, source reads *amorosa* for *amoroso;* lines 8–9, these appear in Guarini's text, but are omitted by Caimo.

## [7] *Io piansi un tempo*

| | |
|---|---|
| Io piansi un tempo e fu s'il piant' amaro | I wept for a time, and so bitter was my weeping |
| Che tutto giel' e ghiaccio diventai, | That it was frost and ice that I became; |
| Ma poi cantai subito ch'io arsi. | But then I sang, as soon as I caught fire. |
| O felici sospir' a l'aure sparsi. | Oh, happy sighs, scattered to the breezes! |

NOTE ON THE TEXT: Line 2, source reads *giaccio* for *ghiaccio.*

## [8] *Parto da voi*

| | |
|---|---|
| Parto da voi e so con quanta pena | I leave you, and I know with how much difficulty |
|   Faccio da voi partita, | I take leave of you, |
| Che nel partir da me parte la vita. | For as I leave you, my life leaves me. |
| Parto da voi perchè l'alma et serena | I am leaving you because your dear, serene, |
|   Vostra serena vista | Your serene glance |
|   Hor mi si mostra a torto | Now wrongly shows itself to me |
|   Sì nubilosa e trista; | Clouded and angry; |
| Ma 'n questo dipartir ho un sol conforto, | But in this departure, I have one sole comfort, |
| Ch'io sper' ancor veder pietosi quelli | For I hope once again to see them merciful, |
|   Occhi sereni e belli. | Those serene and lovely eyes. |

## [9] *Mi suggean l'api il mele*

| | |
|---|---|
|   Mi suggean l'api il mele, | The bees formerly sucked their honey from me, |
|   Hor mi tragge l'odore | Now my perfume draws to me |
| Una dolce novella ape d'amore, | A sweet new bee of love; |
|   E par che non m'annoi, | And it seems that she gives me no pain, |
|   Amor, ma che fia poi | Love; but what will happen later, |
| S'ella il candido sen per me s'infiori? | If I am the flower with which she adorns her white breast? |
| | |
| Sarei pur anch' io Re de gl'altri fiori. | I too would be King of the other flowers. |

AUTHOR: Girolamo Casone

POETIC SOURCE: Girolamo Casone, *Rime* (Venice: Gio. Battista Ciotti, 1601 [first publ. 1598]), fol. 15v.

## [10] *Poi che 'l mio largo pianto*

| | |
|---|---|
|   Poi che 'l mio largo pianto, | Since my abundant weeping, |
|   Amor, ti piace tanto, | Love, pleases you so much, |
| Asciutti mai quest' occhi non vedrai | You will never see these eyes dry |
|   Finchè non mandi fuore, | Until you have sent out, |
|   Ohimè, per gl'occh' il cuore. | Alas, this heart through my eyes. |

NOTE ON THE TEXT: Lines 4–5, for an interpretation see the note to [11] "Poi che ne' bei sospiri," below.

## [11] *Poi che ne' bei sospiri*

Poi che ne' bei sospiri,
  Amor, lieto respiri,
Mai non alleviar fiamma sì dolce
  Finchè 'l soave ardore
Non torn' al loco suo, per gl'occh' il core.

Since in my deep sighs,
Love, you breathe so happily,
Never weaken so sweet a flame
Until its gentle burning
Returns to its proper place through the eyes.

NOTE ON THE TEXT: Lines 4–5, in other words, the fire, which is the natural heat of the heart, is being sent out through the eyes by weeping; when the fire has been completely expelled, the speaker will no longer be alive and the fire will have returned to its "proper place," i.e., the sphere of fire.

## [12] *Scoprirò l'ardor mio*

Scoprirò l'ardor mio con dir ch'io moro.
  Fiera stella, empia sorte!
Hai, non fia ver, perchè colui ch'adoro
  Gioisce di mia morte
  E per tormi la vita
  Non mi darebb' aita.

I will reveal my passion, saying that I die.
Cruel star, pitiless fate!
Ah, let it not be true, for he whom I adore
Rejoices in my death
And, in order to take my life,
Would never help me.

*Risposta*

Se voi sete il mio sol, se per voi moro,
  E m'è felice sorte,
Come potrei mirar gl'occhi ch'adoro
  Scoloriti per morte?
  Mi togliete la vita
Con domandarmi aita.

If you are my sun, if for you I die
By happy fate,
How could I gaze on the eyes I adore
If they were discolored by death?
You take away my life
If you ask me for help.

## [13] *Se voi set' il mio cor*

Se voi set' il mio cor, l'alma, e la vita,
  Hor che di voi son privo
  Chi può tenermi vivo?
Deh vita mia, se l'amorosa salma
  Pietà trova tal hora,
  Tornate ch'io non muora.

If you are my heart, my soul, and my life,
Now that I am bereft of you
Who can keep me alive?
Ah, my life, if dead lovers
Do at length find pity,
Return, that I may not die.

NOTE ON THE TEXT: Line 1, in most other settings this reads, "Se voi set' il mio cor, la vita e l'alma," which corrects the rhyme with line 4.

## [14] *Che fa hoggi il mio sole*

Che fa hoggi il mio sole
Che non cantan di lei la gloria e 'l vanto?
  Hor queste mie viole
  Et questi fior gli dono
Che ne facci corona a le sue chiome.

What is my sun doing today
That they are not singing her glory and her praise?
Now these violets of mine
And these flowers I give her,
That she may make a crown of them for her hair.

## [15] *Chi mov' il piè*

*Prima parte*

Chi mov' il piè per quest' oscuri e torti

Sentieri, ov' a cader va l'huom sì spesso
E lunge da quel ben ch'a Dio promesso
Segu' il piacer fra mill' affanni e morti,

Whoever moves his feet through these dark and
  twisted
Paths where men fall so frequently,
And, far from that happiness that God has promised,
Follows pleasure among a thousand labors and
  deaths—

xxxiii

Col chiaro lume di pensieri accorti
E con quanto valor gl'ha Dio concesso
Convien che desti al somm' amor se stesso
Tenend' i sensi castigati e morti.

*Seconda parte*

Perchè 'l raggio divin la via ne mostra
Dritta ch'adduce a fine alto e perfetto,
E de l'alma gl'horrori apre e rischiara;
E 'l sens' afflitto col miglior non giostra,
Ma 'l servo humile ond' il purgat' affetto
A fuggir ogn' error del mond' impara.

By the clear light of thought, once awakened,
And with whatever strength God has granted him,
He must rouse himself to the highest love,
Mortifying and chastening his senses.

For the divine light shows us the straight
Way that leads to a high and perfect goal,
And opens up and soothes the horror of the soul;
Afflicted sense does not fight against the right,
But humbly serves, and thus the purged feelings
Learn to flee every deception of the world.

AUTHOR: Gabriel Fiamma

POETIC SOURCE: Gabriel Fiamma, *Rime spirituali* (Venice: Francesco de' Franceschi Senese, 1560), Sonnet 80.

NOTES ON THE TEXT: *Prima parte,* line 3, source reads *promesse* for *promesso. Seconda parte,* line 4, source reads *ne;* literary source reads *non.*

## [16] *È ben ragion*

È ben ragion se l'eterno mottore
De cieli ha d'aspre spine il capo avinto,

Ch'anco il pianeta che distingue l'hore
Sdegni haver hoggi il suo di raggi cinto.
Et è ragion se l'empio nostro errore
Ha d'ogni luce il fonte, ahi lasso, estinto,
Che d'altra nebbia il mondo anco sia tinto,
Di pioggia gelo e tenebroso horrore.

It is indeed just, if the eternal mover
Of the heavens has bound his head with harsh
    thorns,
That the planet that marks the hours also
Disdains to have his head bound with rays.
And it is just, if our impious error
Has extinguished, alas, the fountain of all light,
That the world also be darkened with another mist,
With rain, with frost, and with dark horrors.

NOTE ON THE TEXT: Lines 1 and 5, source reads *raggion* for *ragion.*

## [17] *Canzone: O sola, o senza par*

*Prima stanza*

O sola, o senza par beata e bella
    Alma real fenice
    Del cui sguardo felice
Arder mia giova e così vuol mia stella,
    Giurai nè temp' o doglia
Fia mai che 'l voto mio d'amarti scioglia.

Oh sole and without equal, blessed and lovely
Beloved regal Phoenix,
In whose happy glance
I love to burn, and thus my star decrees,
I have sworn that neither time nor grief
Will ever cancel my vow to love you.

*Seconda stanza*

Amor vid' io che del suo aurato crine
    Ti coronava, e l'ali
    Di sue penn' immortali
Vestendoti, spargea gratie divine
    Acciò ch'in terra fede
Festi del sommo bel ch'in ciel si vede.

Love I saw, who with his golden locks
Was crowning you, and wings
Of his immortal feathers
Putting on you; he shed divine graces on you
That you might create faith on earth
For the highest beauty that can be seen in heaven.

*Terza stanza*

Sì dolci odori e sì soavi note
    T'usciro all' hor dal petto
    Ch'al novo alto diletto
Fermar il corso le stellanti rote
    E sanno i giusti Dei
Che pur i' ti sacrai gl'affetti miei.

Such sweet perfume and sweet notes
Came forth from your breast then,
That at the new high delight
The starry wheels stood still in their turning,
And the just gods know
That I, too, vowed to you my love.

*Quarta stanza*

| | |
|---|---|
| Come in arido legno il fuoco invia | As in dry wood the fire sends |
| Ratto possente fiamma | A swift, powerful flame |
| Ond' ei tutto s'infiamma | That sets it all afire, |
| E trasformato in lei se stesso oblia, | Transformed to flame, forgetting itself, |
| Così tua viv' imago | So your lively image |
| Cangiò 'l mio cor già del suo incendio vagho. | Has changed my heart, already glad of its burning. |

*Ultima stanza*

| | |
|---|---|
| Cener et ombra è ciò che di me scorgi | Ashes and a shade are what you see of me, |
| Abbandonato in pene, | Abandoned to grief, |
| Che teco l'alma viene | For my soul comes with you, |
| Gloriosa del ben che sent' e porgi, | Glorying in the good that it senses and you offer; |
| E seguend' io tua sorte | And, following your happy lot |
| Vivo vita immortal della mia morte. | I live immortal by my own death. |

NOTES ON THE TEXT: *Terza stanza,* line 1, source reads *notte* in two parts and *notti* in two parts. *Ultima stanza,* line 4, possible translation: "Glorying in the good that you feel and offer."

## *From* Fiamma ardente a 5 (1586)

### [1] *Mirate che m'ha fatto*

| | |
|---|---|
| Mirate che m'ha fatto sto cor mio, | See what this heart of mine has done to me, |
| Che m'è fuggito per seguir la diva | It has fled me to follow the goddess |
| E mormorando và di riva in riva. | And wanders murmuring from shore to shore. |

### [2] *Date la vela al vento*

| | |
|---|---|
| Date la vela al vento, o pensier miei, | Loose the sail to the wind, O my thoughts, |
| Nè temete del mar l'aspra procella | Nor fear the bitter tempest of the sea, |
| Ch'al ben vi scorge tramontana stella. | For the North Star guides you toward the good. |

### [3] *Bene mio, tu m'hai lasciato*

| | |
|---|---|
| Bene mio, tu m'hai lasciato | My love, you have left me |
| Senza speranz' e senz' alcun conforto, | Without hope or any comfort, |
| E poi non vuoi che per te resti morto. | And then you do not want me to die for you. |
| Sì, morirò cor mio, | Yes, I shall die, my heart, |
| Deh, non mi far morire. | Ah, do not make me die. |

### [4] *Un' ape esser vorei*

| | |
|---|---|
| Un' ape esser vorei | I would I were a bee, |
| Poi che vi fece la natura fiore, | Since nature made you a flower, |
| Clori, mia bella, ch'io poi cercarei | My lovely Cloris, for I would seek |
| Per forz' o per inganni, | By force or by deception, |
| Pascermi del soave vostr' odore | To feed on your sweet fragrance, |
| Lasciando questo cor nel vostro còre. | Leaving this heart within your heart. |

NOTE ON THE TEXT: Line 1 is identical with one by Torquato Tasso; see Angelo Solerti, ed., *Le Rime di Torquato Tasso,* vol. 2 (Bologna: Romagnoli-Dall' Acqua, 1898), 512 ("Rime amorose" no. 112).

### [5] *Gioia mia dolc' e cara*

| | |
|---|---|
| Gioia mia dolc' e cara, | My dear sweet joy, |
| Tu sai ch'io t'amo con sincero core. | You know I love you with a sincere heart. |
| Ella con voce chiara, | She, with clear voice, replied, |
| "Sì, 'l so," rispose, "che mi port' amore." | "Yes, I know that you love me." |

NOTE ON THE TEXT: Line 4, source reads *Se* for *Sì.*

## [6] *Dolci sospir'*

| | |
|---|---|
| Dolci sospir', o donna, e dolci pianti, | Sweet sighs, Lady, and sweet weeping, |
| Dolci rancor' e dolci sdegn' et ire, | Sweet grudges, and sweet disdains and anger, |
| Dolcemente mi fa per voi morire. | Sweetly make me die for you. |

## [7] *Lo core mio*

| | |
|---|---|
| Lo core mio è fatt' un Mongibello | My heart has become an Aetna |
| Che giorn' e notte batte lo martello, | That day and night strikes with its hammer |
| Tic e toc, | Tic-toc, |
| Mira, Signora, l'aspro mio dolore | See, Lady, my harsh sorrow, |
| Ch'infern' è fatto per te lo mio core. | For my heart has become a hell on account of you. |

NOTE ON THE TEXT: Lines 1–2, the god Vulcan traditionally had his forge beneath Mt. Aetna.

## [8] *Vola, vola pensier*

| | |
|---|---|
| Vola, vola, pensier, fuor del mio petto, | Fly, fly, my thought, forth from my breast, |
| Vanne veloce a quella faccia bella | Go swiftly to the lovely face |
| Della mia chiara stella, | Of my bright star, |
| Dilli cortesemente e con amore: | Tell her [him?] courteously and with love: |
| Eccoti lo mio core. | Here is my heart for you. |

*Risposta*

| | |
|---|---|
| Torna, torna, pensier, dentr' al mio petto, | Return, return, my thought, into my breast, |
| Lascia veloce a quella faccia bella | Quickly leave the lovely face |
| Che fa mia chiara stella | Of my bright star |
| Dilli ch'acceso sei di nov' ardore: | Tell her [him?], since you are aflame with new ardor: |
| Rendimi lo mio core. | Give me back my heart. |

AUTHOR: Torquato Tasso

POETIC SOURCE: Torquato Tasso, *Rime inedite o disperse*, ed. Gio. Rosini, Opere di Torquato Tasso 32 (Pisa: Niccolò Capurro, 1831), 95.

NOTES ON THE TEXT: Lines 1–5 are the beginning of a longer madrigal by Tasso; Angelo Solerti, ed., *Le Rime di Torquato Tasso*, vol. 1 (Bologna: Romangnoli-Dall' Acqua, 1898), 118, 122, 123, and 125 cites five manuscript sources containing the poem; a number of nineteenth-century printed collections also contain the work (see, for example, ibid., 327, 329, 331, 354, 366, 369, and 372 as well as the Poetic Source above. In a listing of musical collections containing Tasso's poems, Solerti implies that the *risposta* is also by Tasso (ibid., 441). Line 4, Tasso's original has a feminine pronoun here. *Risposta*, line 4, source reads *ch'accesa* for *ch'acceso*.

## [9] *Tutte l'offese*

| | |
|---|---|
| Tutte l'offese che m'hai fatt', Amore | All the injuries that you have done me, Love, |
| Io ti perdono pur c'habbi giurato | I will forgive as soon as you have sworn |
| Di mai più farmi star inamorato. | Never to make me fall in love again. |

## [10] *Canzone: Partomi, donna*

*Prima parte*

| | |
|---|---|
| Partomi, donna, e teco lascio il core | I leave you, Lady, and leave my heart with you |
| Per pegno de mia fe constant' e forte, | As a pledge of my constant, strong troth, |
| Che sempre tuo sarò fin' alla morte. | For I will be always yours till death. |

*Seconda parte*

| | |
|---|---|
| Il cor e l'alma crepa di dolore | My heart and soul are dying of grief |
| Partirmi senza te, dolce mio bene, | Since I depart without you, my sweet love, |
| Che sempre viverò in doglia e pene. | For always I will live in sorrow and suffering. |

*Terza parte*

Forz' è ch'io parti e non posso partire
Senza vederti, o mio dolce conforto;
Consoli questo cor già quasi morto.

I must go but I cannot go
Without seeing you, O my sweet comfort;
Console this heart that is already almost dead.

*Quarta et ultima parte*

Haimè, meschino, mi sento morire
Per la partenza che mi lev' il core:
Ricordati di me, dolce mio Amore.

Ay me, wretch, I feel myself dying
In this departure that takes my heart away:
Remember me, O my sweet love.

NOTE ON THE TEXT: *Seconda parte,* line 1, source reads *creppa* for *crepa.*

## [11] *Occhi leggiadri*

Occhi leggiadri e cari,
Occhi nel mondo rari,
Occhi de l'alma mia fido conforto,
Voi, voi, dolce occhi, voi m'havete morto.

Sparkling dear eyes,
Eyes rare in the world,
Eyes, the faithful comfort of my soul,
You, you, sweet eyes, you have killed me.

NOTE ON THE TEXT: Line 4, source reads *dolc' occhi* for *dolce occhi.*

## [12] *Questa crudel*

Questa crudel ch'adoro,
Pascendosi ogn' hor del mio martire,
Pensa farmi morire,
Ma van' è'l suo pensiero,
Che mentre viverà delli miei guai
Non morirò già mai.

This cruel one whom I adore,
Feeding ever on my suffering,
Thinks to cause my death;
But vain is her thought,
For as long as my woes give her life,
I will never die.

## [13] *'Na volta m'hai gabbato*

'Na volta m'hai gabbato, o ladroncella,
Per la mia bona fe ch'io ti portai,
Ma più non mi ci gabbi a fe già mai.

You tricked me one time, you little thief,
Because of the trust I placed in you,
But you will never mock my trust again.

NOTES ON THE TEXT: Line 1, source reads *gabat'* for *gabbato.* Line 3, source reads *gabi* for *gabbi.*

## [14] *Con tue lusinghe, Amore*

Con tue lusinghe, Amore,
Sai quante volte m'hai rubato il core,

Mostrandoti al principio dolc' e pio,
Poi nella fin sempre crudel e rio.

With your flatteries, Love,
You know how many times you have stolen my
    heart,
Making show at the outset to be sweet and merciful,
Then at the end always cruel and pitiless.

PLATE 1. Canto part of [7] "Se potesse morir" from the *Madrigali a 4*, showing the musical pun on the text "fra mille mort' io non potrei morire" ("amid a thousand deaths I could not die"). The poet's inability to die is mirrored by the composer's inability to properly cadence; the rests and *custos* at the end of the piece imply more music to come. (N.B.: Luigi Cassola's text is incorrectly printed in Caimo's collection as "Se potesse mirar." See Texts and Translations.)
Reprinted by permission of the British Library.

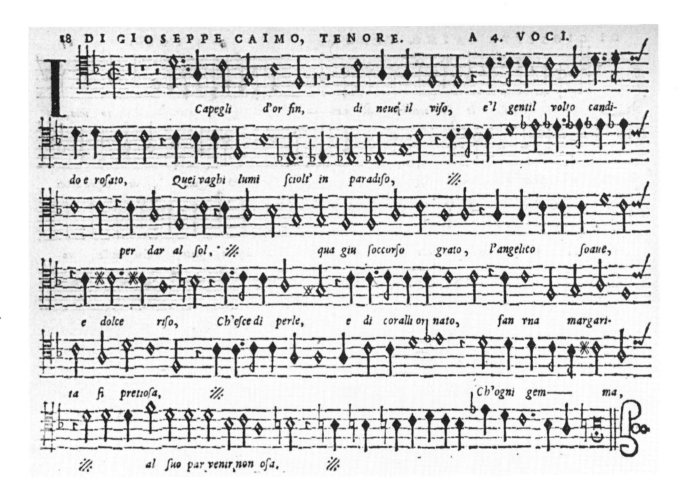

PLATE 2. Tenor part of [9] "I capegli d'or fin" from the *Madrigali a 4*, showing the editorial policy of the publisher, Francesco Moscheni. Successive inflected notes on the same pitch all bear explicit accidentals (see discussion, p. xiii). Reprinted by permission of the British Library.

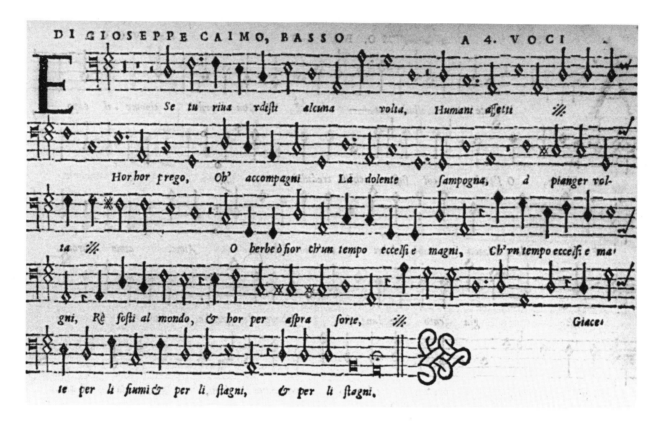

PLATE 3. Bass part of [12] "E se tu, riva, udisti" from the *Madrigali a 4*. That the c-sharp in the second system and the f-sharp in the third system affect only the note immediately following is confirmed by perfect consonances in other voices (see discussion, p. xiv). Compare the fourth system, where the publisher carefully reiterates the sharp for each affected pitch. Reprinted by permission of the British Library.

PLATE 4. Alto part of [5] Gel' ha madonna il core" from the *Madrigali a 5*, showing the editorial policies of the publishers Giacomo Vincenzi and Ricciardo Amadino. The explicit f'-sharp at the beginning of the third system applies to the succeeding five f's as well (see discussion, p. xiv). Reprinted by permission of the Bayerische Staatsbibliothek, Munich.

CANTO

# FIAMMA ARDENTE

## DE MADRIGALI ET CANZONI
### à Cinque Voci,

Con vn Dialogo à Dieci de diuerſi ſoggetti, nouamance
raccolte, & datte in luce, per Gio:Battiſta
Portio Nouareſe.

IN VENETIA
Preſſo Giacomo Vincenzi, & Ricciardo Amadino, compagni

M D LXXXVI.
A inſtantia di Pietro Tini.

PLATE 5. Title page of the canto part of the collection *Fiamma ardente*. Reprinted by permission of the Library of Congress.

# Book 1, Madrigali a 4 (1564)

# [1] Non vide Febo mai

*Madrigali a 4 (1564)*

4

di bel- lez- za, on- de re- stau- ro Stan- ca na- tu- ra

di ver- tù, di bel- lez- za, on- de re- stau- ro Stan- ca na-

di bel- lez- za, on- de re- stau- ro Stan-

-tù, di bel- lez- za, on- de re- stau- ro

pren- de, ⟨stan- ca na- tu- ra pren- de⟩ nel su- o tem- pio,

-tu- ra pren- de nel su- o tem- pio, ⟨nel su- o tem-

-ca na- tu- ra pren- de nel su- o tem- pio, nel su- o tem- pio,

Stan- ca na- tu- ra pren- de nel su- o tem- pio, ⟨nel

⟨nel su- o tem- pio.⟩ Mi- ran- do

-pio, nel su- o tem- pio.⟩ Mi- ran- do la de-gn'o- pra, ⟨mi-

⟨nel su- o tem- pio.⟩ Mi- ran- do la de-gn'o-

su- o tem- pio.⟩ Mi-

la de-gn'o- pra, ⟨mi- ran- do la de-gn'o-
-ran- do la de-gn'o- pra, mi- ran- do la de- gn'o- pra⟩
-pra, ⟨mi- ran- do la de-gn'o- pra⟩
-ran- do la de-gn'o- pra, ⟨mi- ran- do la de-gn'o- pra⟩

-pra⟩ e'l bel the-sau- ro, ⟨e'l bel the-sau- ro,⟩ In- vi- dia pu- gne A-mor la-
e'l bel the-sau- ro, ⟨e'l bel the-sau- ro,⟩ In- vi- dia pu- gne A-mor
e'l bel the-sau- ro, ⟨e'l bel the- sau- ro,⟩ In- vi- dia pu- gne A-mor
e'l bel the-sau- ro, ⟨e'l bel the-sau- ro,⟩ In- vi- dia pu- gne A-mor

-sci-vo et em- pio, ⟨la- sci-vo et em- pio,⟩ Ma Lu- do- vi-
la- sci- vo et em- pio, la- sci-vo et em- pio, Ma Lu- do-
la- sci-vo et em- pio, ⟨la- sci-vo et em- pio,⟩ Ma
la- sci- vo et em- pio, ⟨la- sci-vo et em- pio,⟩ Ma

-co̱ a sè_____ su a- ve̱ il pie- ga, ⟨ma Lu- do- vi-

-vi- co̱ a sè_____ su a- ve̱ il pie- ga, ⟨ma

Lu- do- vi- co̱ a sè su- a- ve̱ il pie- ga,

Lu- do- vi- co̱ a sè su- a- ve̱ il pie- ga ⟨ma Lu- do-

-co̱ a sè su a- ve̱ il pie- ga,⟩ E Por- tia col_____ bel crin lo

Lu- do- vi- co̱ a sè su- a- ve̱ il pie- ga,⟩ E Por- tia col_____ bel crin lo

⟨ma Lu- do- vi- co̱ a sè su- a- ve̱ il pie- ga,⟩ E Por- tia col_____ bel crin lo

-vi- co̱ a sè su- a- ve̱ il pie- ga,⟩ E Por- tia col_____ bel crin lo

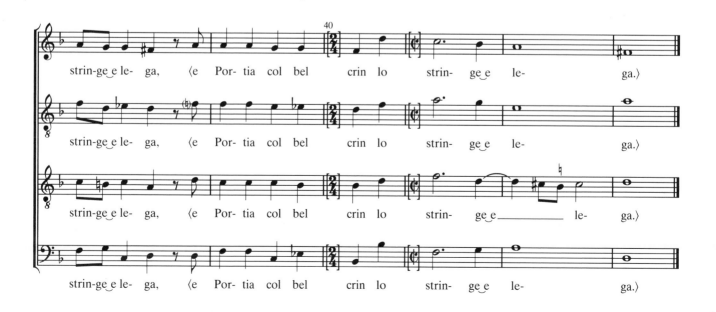

strin- ge̱ e̱ le- ga, ⟨e Por- tia col bel crin lo strin- ge̱ e le- ga.⟩

strin- ge̱ e̱ le- ga, ⟨e Por- tia col bel crin lo strin- ge̱ e le- ga.⟩

strin- ge̱ e̱ le- ga, ⟨e Por- tia col bel crin lo strin- ge̱ e_____ le- ga.⟩

strin- ge̱ e̱ le- ga, ⟨e Por- tia col bel crin lo strin- ge̱ e le- ga.⟩

# [2] Stando per maraviglia

Jacopo Sannazaro

*Madrigali a 4 (1564)*

-scio dal cie- - lo, Per far- mi pri- vo, ⟨per far- mi pri- vo⟩ on-d'e- ra

dal ciel- - lo, Per far- mi pri- vo, ⟨per far-mi pri- vo⟩ on-d'e- ra

- scio dal cie- - lo, Per far- mi pri- vo, ⟨per far-mi pri- vo⟩ on-d'e- ra

-scio dal cie- - lo, Per far- mi pri- vo, ⟨per far-mi pri- vo⟩ on-d'e- ra

sì di- vi- - so.                                     Qual nuo-va in- vi-

sì di- vi- so. Qual nuo-va in- vi-dia è na-ta in pa- ra- di- so, ⟨qual nuo-va in-

sì di- vi- so. Qual nuo-va in- vi-dia è na-ta in pa- ra- di- so, ⟨qual nuo-va in-vi-

sì di- vi- so. Qual nuo-va in- vi-dia è na-ta in pa- ra- di- so, ⟨qual nuo-va in-

-dia è na- ta in pa- ra- di- so, Ac- ciò che in-nan- z'il tem- po io can-

-vi- dia è na- ta in pa- ra- di- so,⟩ Ac-ciò che in- nan-z'il tem- po io can-g'il pe- lo, io

-dia è na- ta in pa- ra- di- so,⟩ Ac- ciò che in- nan- z'il tem-po io

-vi- dia è na- ta in pa- ra- di- so,⟩ Ac- ciò che in- nan-z'il tem-po io

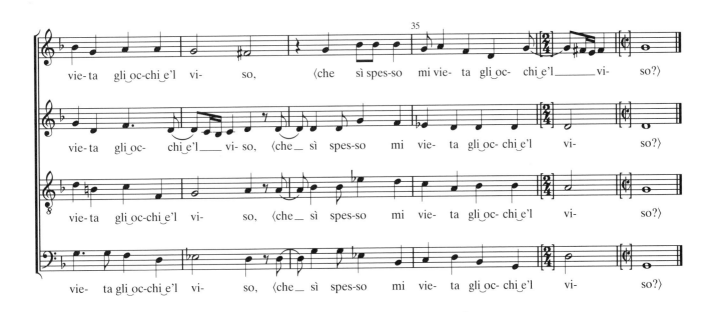

10

**Seconda parte**

*Alto should sing an eighth note here. See discussion in Preface, p. xiv.

12

# [3] Gratia non vider mai

*Madrigali a 4 (1564)*

14

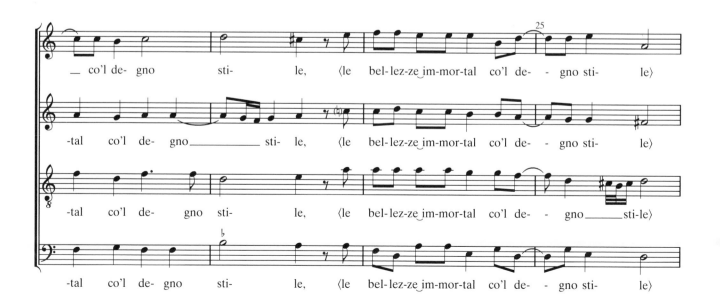

Gl'al-tier co- stu- mi che da Bat- tro a Ti- le Ri- suo- nan, m'han sup-po-sto al-

Gl'al-tier co- stu- mi che da Bat- tro a Ti- le Ri- suo- nan, m'han sup-po-sto al-

Gl'al-tier co- stu- mi che da Bat-tro a Ti- le Ri- suo- nan, m'han sup-po-sto al-

Gl'al-tier co- stu- mi che da Bat-tro a Ti- le Ri- suo- nan, m'han sup-po-sto al-

-li su'o-me- i, ⟨ri- suo-nan, m'han sup- po-sto al-li su'o- me- i.⟩

-li su'o- me- i, ⟨ri- suo-nan, m'han sup- po-sto al-li su'o- me- i.⟩

-li su'o-me- i, ⟨ri- suo-nan, m'han sup- po-sto al-li su'o- me- i.⟩

-li su'o-me- i, ⟨ri- suo-nan, m'han sup- po-sto al-li su'o- me- i.⟩

**Seconda parte**

Sì che____ non bra-

Sì che____ non bra- mo, ⟨sì che____ non____ bra-

Sì che____ non____ bra- mo, ⟨sì che____ non bra-

Sì che____ non bra- mo,

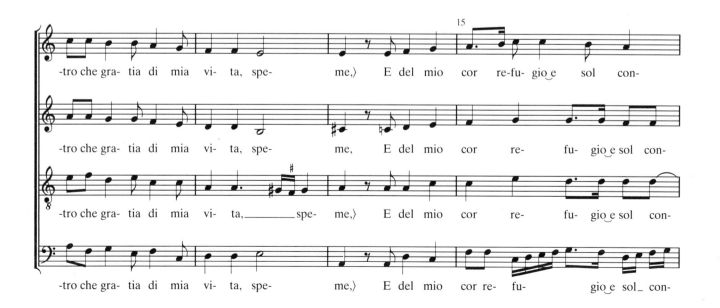

-ten- to, Pe- rò non sia don-n'al- tra che m'af- -fer- ra Con

-ten- to, Pe- rò non sia don-n'al- tra che,_____ m'af- fer- ra Con

- ten- to, Pe- rò non_____ sia don-n'al- tra_____ che___ m'af- fer- ra Con

-ten- to, Pe- rò non sia don-n'al- tra che_____ m'af- fer- ra Con

su- a bel- lez- za il cuor_ e l'al-ma in- sie- me, Che pri- a vor-rò es- ser_

su- a bel- lez- za il cuor e l'al- ma in-sie- me, Che pri- a vor-rò es- ser di,_

su- a bel- lez- za il cuor e l'al- ma in - sie- me, Che pri- a vor-rò es- ser di,_

su- a bel- lez- za il cuor e l'al-ma in- sie- me, Che pri- a vor-rò es- ser di,_

_ di vi- ta spen- to, ⟨che pri- a vor- rò es- ser di vi- ta spen- to.⟩

_ di vi- ta_____ spen- to, che pri- a vor-rò es- ser di vi- ta spen- to.

_ [di] vi- ta spen- to, ⟨che pri- a vor- rò es- ser di vi- ta_____ spen- to.⟩

_ di vi- ta spen- to, ⟨che pri- a vor- rò es- ser di vi- ta spen- to.⟩

# [4] Qual gratia sparse mai

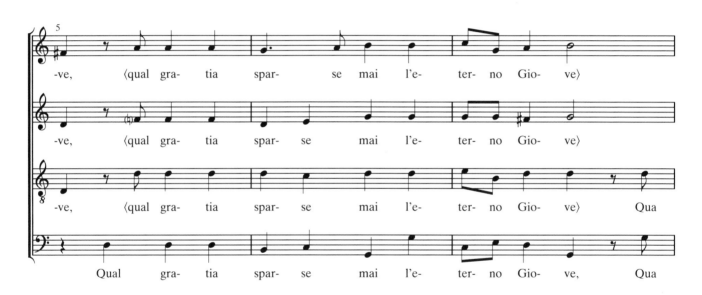

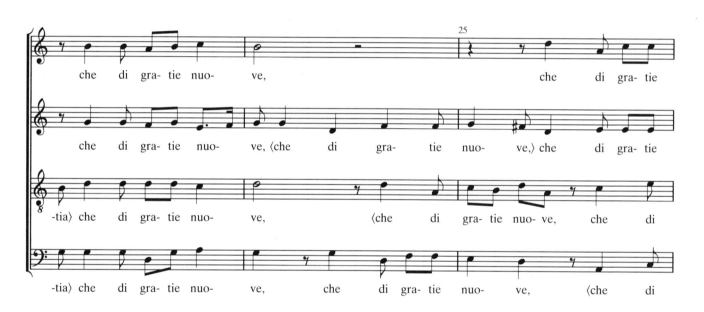

-li! O- di Ec- - cho ri- suo-nar tut- te le_____ va- li: "Gra-

-li! O- di Ec- - cho ri- suo-nar tut- te le va- li: "Gra-

-li! O- di Ec- - cho ri- suo-nar tut- te le va- li:

-li! O- di Ec- - cho ri- suo-nar tut- te le va- li:

- tia, ⟨gra- tia, gra- - tia⟩ e bel- tà d'o- gn'u- no muo- ve."

-tia, ⟨gra- tia,⟩ gra- tia e bel- tà d'o- gn'u- no_____ muo- ve."

"Gra- tia, ⟨gra- tia, gra- tia⟩ e bel- tà d'o- gn'u- no muo- ve."

"Gra- tia, ⟨gra- tia,⟩ gra- tia e bel- tà d'o- gn'u- no muo- ve."

**Seconda parte**

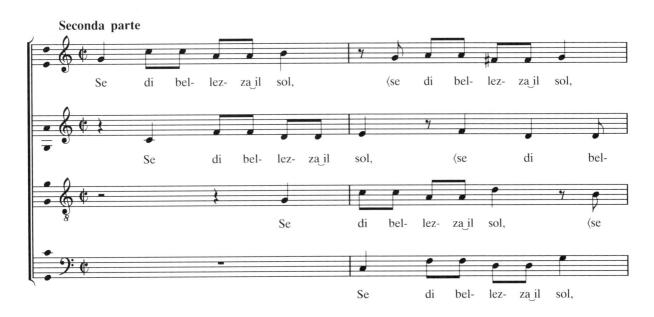

Se di bel- lez- za il sol, ⟨se di bel- lez- za il sol,

Se di bel- lez- za il sol, ⟨se di bel-

Se di bel- lez- za il sol, ⟨se

Se di bel- lez- za il sol,

22

se di bel- lez- za il sol,⟩ di Gra- tia Giu- no A- van-

-lez- za il sol, se di bel- lez- za il sol,⟩ di Gra- tia Giu- no A- van-

di bel- lez- za il sol,⟩ di Gra- tia Giu- no A- van-

⟨se di bel- lez- za il sol,⟩ di Gra- tia Giu- no A- van-

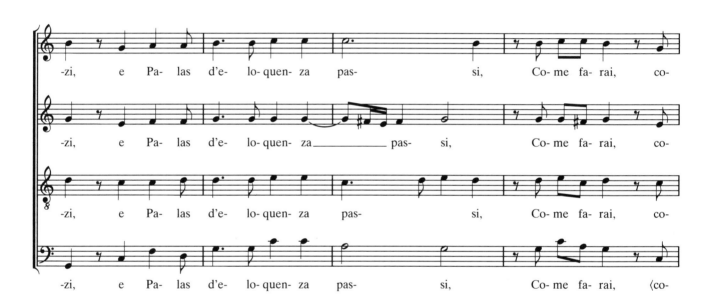

-zi, e Pa- las d'e- lo- quen- za pas- si, Co- me fa- rai, co-

-zi, e Pa- las d'e- lo- quen- za_____ pas- si, Co- me fa- rai, co-

-zi, e Pa- las d'e- lo- quen- za pas- si, Co- me fa- rai, co-

-zi, e Pa- las d'e- lo- quen- za pas- si, Co- me fa- rai, ⟨co-

-me fa- rai ch'in te Gra- tia non tro- vi, ch'in te Gra- tia non tro- vi, ⟨ch'in

-me fa- rai ch'in te Gra- tia non tro- vi, ch'in te Gra- tia non tro- vi, ⟨ch'in

-me fa- rai ch'in te Gra- tia non tro- vi, ch'in te Gra- tia non tro- vi, ⟨ch'in

-me fa- rai⟩ ch'in te Gra- tia non tro- vi, ch'in te Gra- tia non tro- vi, ⟨ch'in

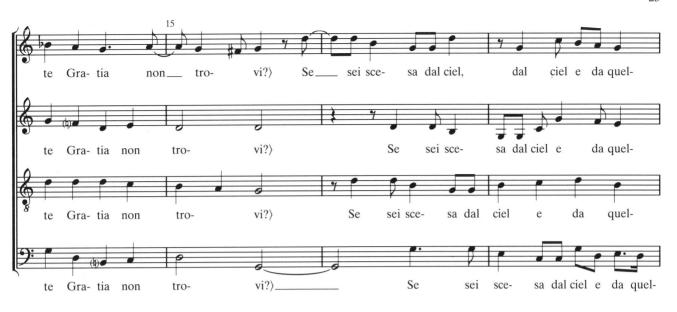

te Gra- tia non\_ tro- vi?⟩ Se\_ sei sce- sa dal ciel, dal ciel e da quel-

te Gra- tia non tro- vi?⟩ Se sei sce- sa dal ciel e da quel-

te Gra- tia non tro- vi?⟩ Se sei sce- sa dal ciel e da quel-

te Gra- tia non tro- vi?⟩\_ Se sei sce- sa dal ciel e da quel-

-l'u- no E\_ tri- no Gio-ve\_or-na- ta, hai- mè,\_ non las-

-l'u- no E\_ tri- no Gio-ve\_or-na- ta, hai- mè,\_ non las-

-l'u- no E\_ tri- no Gio-ve\_or-na- ta, hai- mè,\_ non las-

-l'u- no E\_ tri- no Gio-ve\_or-na- ta, hai- mè,\_ non las-

-si A- die- tro\_o- gn'al- tra, deh\_ pie- tà ti muo- vi.

-si A- die- tro\_o- gn'al- tra, deh\_ pie- tà ti muo- vi.

-si A- die- tro\_o- gn'al- tra, deh\_ pie- tà ti muo- vi.

-si A- die- tro\_o- gn'al- tra, deh\_ pie- tà ti muo- vi.

# [5] Eccelsa e generosa prole

*Alli figliuoli del Sereniss. Rè Massimigliano d'Austria*

[Prima parte]

Madrigali a 4 (1564)

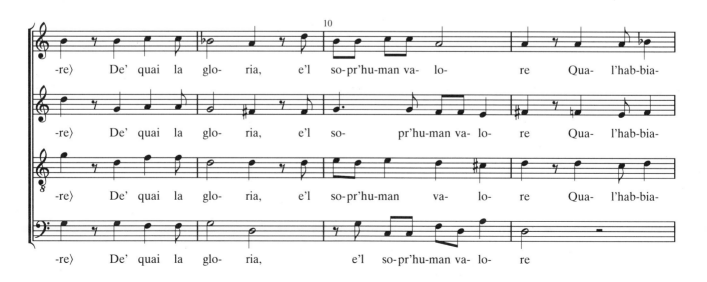

-te a se- guir, ⟨qua- l'hab- bia- te a se- guir⟩ sen- tier v'in- se- gna, qua- l'hab- bia-

-te a se- guir, ⟨qua- l'hab- bia- te a se- guir⟩ sen- tier v'in - se- gna, ⟨qua- l'hab- bia-

-te a se- guir, ⟨qua- l'hab- bia- te a se- guir⟩ sen- tier v'in- se- gna, qua- l'hab- bia-

-te a se- guir sen- tier v'in- se- gna, Sia- - vi ad o- gn'hor___ più a- mi-

-te a se- guir sen- tier v'in - se- gna,⟩ Sia- - vi ad o- gn'hor___ più a- mi-

-te a se- guir sen- tier v'in- se- gna, Sia- - vi ad o- gn'hor___ più a- mi-

Sia- - vi ad o- gn'hor___ più a- mi-

- ca e più___ be- ni- gna O- gni stel - la del ciel co'l

- ca e più___ be- ni- gna O- gni stel - la del ciel co'l

- ca e più___ be- ni- gna O- gni stel - la del ciel co'l

- ca e più___ be- ni- gna O- gni stel - la del ciel co'l

cui fa- vo- re Lie- ti nel sen v'ac-col- ga, an-zi nel co- re, L'al- to zio

cui fa- vo- re Lie- ti nel sen v'ac-col- ga, an-zi nel co- re, L'al- to zio

cui fa- vo- re Lie- ti nel sen v'ac-col- ga, an-zi nel co- re, L'al- to zio

cui fa- vo- re Lie- ti nel sen v'ac-col- ga, an-zi nel co- re, L'al- to zio

vo- stro ch'in I- spa- gna re- gna, ch'in I- spa-gna re- gna.

vo- stro ch'in I- spa- gna re- gna, ch'in I- spa- gna re- gna.

vo- stro ch'in I- spa- gna re- gna, ch'in I- spa- gna re- gna.

vo- stro ch'in I- spa- gna re- gna, ch'in I- spa-gna re- gna.

**Seconda parte**

Sot- to l'om- bra del qual sì cre- sce in vo-

Sot- to l'om- bra del qual sì cre-

Sot- to l'om- bra del qual sì

Sot- to l'om- bra del

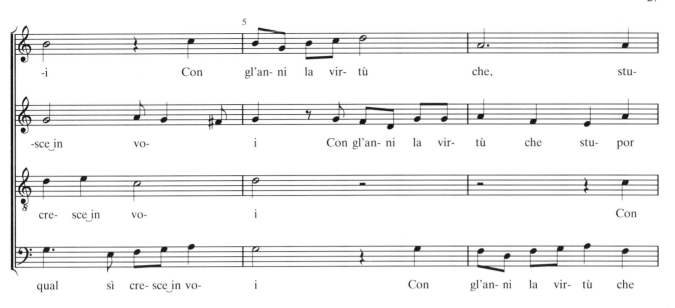

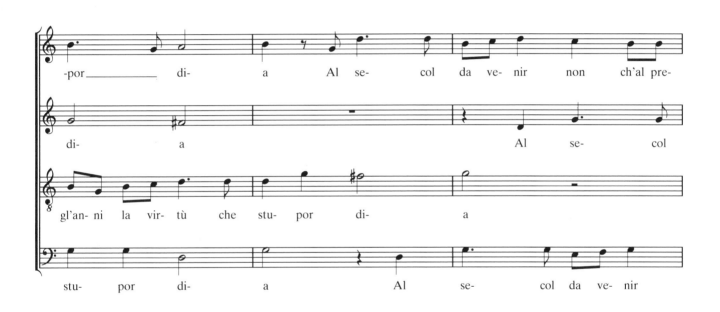

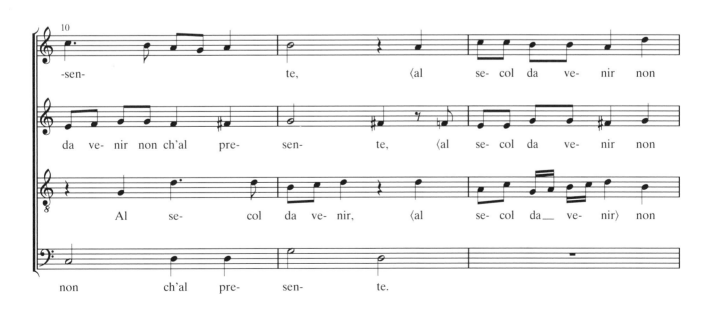

ch'al pre- sen- te.⟩ Giun-ti a l'e- tà del ve-stir l'ar- mi_____ po- i, ⟨giun-ti a l'e- tà del

ch'al pre- sen- te.⟩ Giun-ti a l'e- tà del ve-stir l'ar-mi po- i, giun-ti a l'e- tà del

ch'al pre- sen- te. Giun-ti a l'e- tà del ve-stir l'ar-mi po- i, giun-ti a l'e- tà del

Giun- ti a l'e- tà del_____ ve-stir l'ar-mi po- i

ve- stir l'ar- mi po- i⟩ La for- z'e'l sen- no tal, ⟨la for-

ve- stir l'ar- mi_____ po- i La for- z'e'l sen- no tal, ⟨la for-

ve- stir l'ar- mi po- i La for- z'e'l sen- no tal, ⟨la for-

La for- z'e'l sen- no tal, ⟨la for-

-z'e'l sen- no tal,⟩ tal l'ar- dir si- a Ch'i- nal- zi Eu-

-z'e'l sen- no tal,⟩ tal l'ar- dir si- a Ch'i- nal- zi

-z'e'l sen- no tal,⟩ tal l'ar- dir_____ si- a

-z'e'l sen- no tal,⟩ tal l'ar- dir si- a Ch'i-

-ro- pa e fac- cia A- sia do- len- te, A- sia do- len- te.

Eu- ro-pa e fac- cia A- sia do- len- te, A- sia do- len- te.

Ch'i-nal- zi Eu- ro-pa e fac-cia A-sia do- len- te, A- sia do- len- te.

-nal- zi Eu- ro- pa e fac-cia A-sia do- len- te, A- sia do- len- te.

# [6] Chi vuol veder in terra

*Madrigali a 4 (1564)*

Mi- ri co- stei, ⟨mi- ri co- stei⟩ ch'[è] un sol al pa-rer mi- o.

-o⟩ Mi- ri co- stei, ⟨mi- ri co-stei⟩ ch'[è] un sol al pa-rer mi- o.

-o⟩ Mi- ri co-stei, ⟨mi- ri co- stei⟩ ch'[è] un sol al pa-rer mi- o.

-o Mi- ri co- stei, ⟨mi- ri co-stei⟩ ch'[è] un sol al pa-rer mi- o.

**Seconda parte**

El- la coi rai at- ter- ra O- gni vi- sta mor-

El- la coi rai at- ter- ra, ⟨el- la coi rai at- ter-

El- la coi rai at- ter- ra O- gni

El- la coi rai at- - ter- ra

-tal co- me far suo- le, co- me far suo- le

-ra⟩ O- gni vi- sta mor- tal co-me far suo- le

vi- sta mor- tal co- me_____ far_____ suo- le

O- gni vi- sta mor- tal co- me far suo- le

Gra- tia che vie- n'in-nan- zi al nuo-vo so- le, Gra- tia che vie- n'in-nan- zi al nuo-vo so-

Gra- tia che vie- n'in-nan- zi al nuo-vo so- le, Gra- tia che vie- n'in-nan- zi al nuo-vo so-

Gra- tia che vie- n'in-nan- zi al nuo-vo so- le, Gra- tia che vie- n'in-nan- zi al nuo-vo so-

Gra- tia che vie- n'in-nan- zi al nuo-vo so- le, Gra- tia che vie- n'in-nan- zi al nuo-vo so-

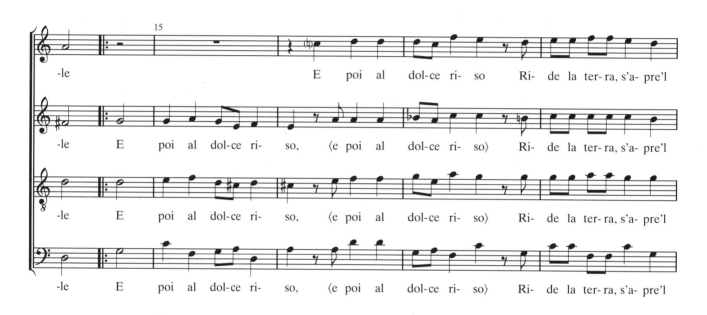

-le E poi al dol-ce ri- so Ri- de la ter- ra, s'a- pre'l

-le E poi al dol-ce ri- so, ⟨e poi al dol-ce ri- so⟩ Ri- de la ter- ra, s'a- pre'l

-le E poi al dol-ce ri- so, ⟨e poi al dol-ce ri- so⟩ Ri- de la ter- ra, s'a- pre'l

-le E poi al dol-ce ri- so, ⟨e poi al dol-ce ri- so⟩ Ri- de la ter- ra, s'a- pre'l

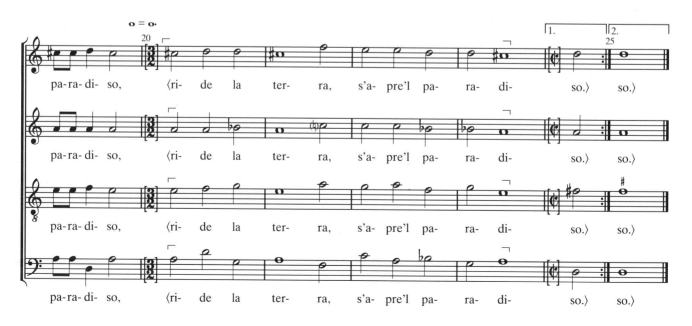

pa- ra- di- so, ⟨ri- de la ter- ra, s'a- pre'l pa- ra- di- so.⟩ so.⟩

pa- ra- di- so, ⟨ri- de la ter- ra, s'a- pre'l pa- ra- di- so.⟩ so.⟩

pa- ra- di- so, ⟨ri- de la ter- ra, s'a- pre'l pa- ra- di- so.⟩ so.⟩

pa- ra- di- so, ⟨ri- de la ter- ra, s'a- pre'l pa- ra- di- so.⟩ so.⟩

# [7] Se potesse morir

Luigi Cassola

*Madrigali a 4 (1654)*

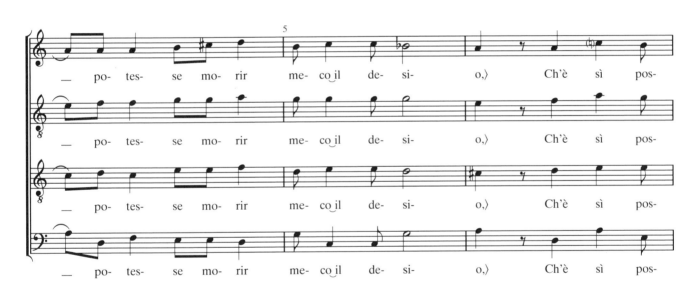

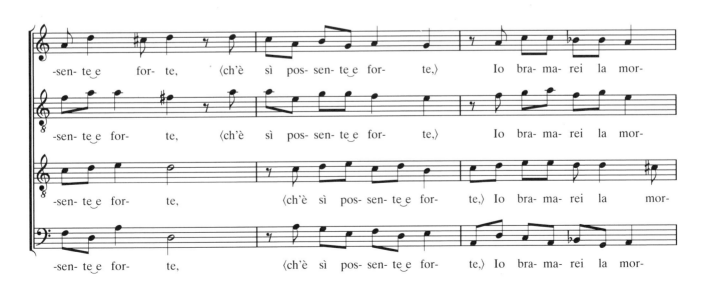

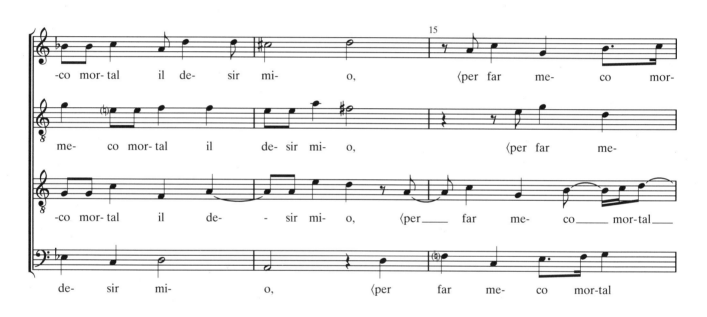

-re, ⟨nè per lie- to___ gio- i- re,⟩ Fra mil- le mor- t'io non po- trei mo-

-re, nè per lie- to___ gio- i- re, Fra mil- le mor- t'io non po- trei mo-

-re, nè per lie- to___ gio- i- re, Fra mil- le mor- t'io non po- trei mo-

nè per lie- to___ gio- i- re, Fra mil- le mor- t'io non po- trei mo-

-ri- re, ⟨fra mil- le mor- t'io non po- trei mo- ri- re.⟩

-ri- re, ⟨fra mil- le mor- t'io non po- trei mo- ri- re.⟩

-ri- re, ⟨fra mil- le mor- t'io non po- trei mo- ri- re.⟩

-ri- re, ⟨fra mil- le mor- t'io non po- trei mo- ri- re.⟩

# [8] Sestina: Che pro mi vien

Bernardo Tasso

**[Prima parte]**

*Madrigali a 4 (1564)*

Canto: Che pro mi vien, ⟨che pro mi vien⟩

Alto: Che pro mi vien, ⟨che pro mi vien⟩ ch'io

Tenore: Che pro mi vien, ⟨che pro mi vien⟩ ch'io

Basso: Che pro mi vien, ⟨che pro mi vien⟩

Canto: ch'io t'ab- bia, o bel- la di- va, ⟨ch'io t'ab- bia, o bel- la di- va⟩

Alto: t'ab- bia, o bel- la di - va, ⟨ch'io t'ab-bia, o bel- la di- va⟩

Tenore: t'ab- bia, o bel- la di- va, ⟨ch'io t'ab-bia, o bel- la di- va⟩ Che reg- gi'l

Basso: ch'io t'ab- bia, o bel- la di- va, Che reg- gi'l

Canto: Che reg- gi'l ter- zo cie- lo, Su que- sta ver- d'e

Alto: Che reg- gi'l ter- zo cie- lo, il ter- zo cie- lo, Su que- sta ver- d'e

Tenore: ter- zo cie- lo, ⟨che reg- gi'l ter- zo cie- lo,⟩ Su que- sta ver- d'e

Basso: ter- zo cie- lo, il ter- zo cie- lo, Su que- sta ver- d'e

di- let- to- sa ri- va, ⟨su que- sta ver- d'e di- let- to- sa

di- let- to- sa ri- va, ⟨su que- sta ver- d'e di- let- to- sa____

di- let- to- sa ri- va, ⟨su que- sta ver- d'e di- let- to- sa

di- let- to- sa ri- va, ⟨su que- sta ver- d'e di- let- to- sa

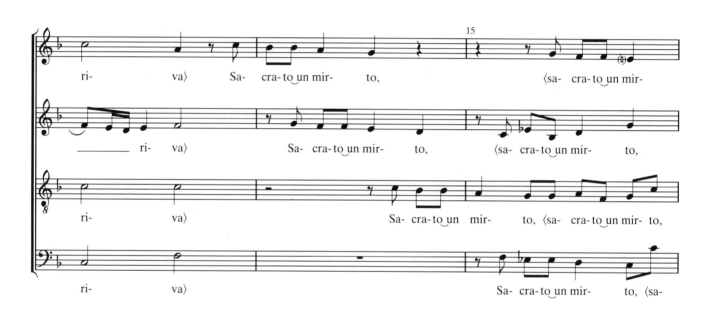

ri- va⟩ Sa- cra- to un mir- to, ⟨sa- cra- to un mir-

____ ri- va⟩ Sa- cra- to un mir- to, ⟨sa- cra- to un mir- to,

ri- va⟩ Sa- cra- to un mir- to, ⟨sa- cra- to un mir- to,

ri- va⟩ Sa- cra- to un mir- to, ⟨sa-

-to, sa- cra- to un mir- to⟩ il cui fron-

sa- cra- to un mir- to,⟩ sa- cra- to un____ mir- to il cui fron-

sa- cra- to un mir- to,⟩ sa- cra- to un mir- to il cui fron-

-cra- to un mir- to,⟩ sa- cra- to un mir- to il cui fron-

-do- so cri- ne  Non te- me i- ra, non te- me i- ra di ghiac-ci'o

-do- so cri- ne  Non te- me i- ra, non te- me i- ra di ghiac- ci'o

-do- so cri- ne  Non te- me i- ra, non te- me i- ra di ghiac- ci'o

-do- so cri- ne  Non te- me i- ra,

di pru- i- ne, ⟨non te- me i- ra di ghiac-ci'o di pru- i- ne?⟩

di pru- i- ne, ⟨non te- me i- ra di ghiac-ci'o di pru- i- ne?⟩

di pru- i- ne, ⟨non te- me i- ra di ghiac-ci'o di pru- i- ne?⟩

⟨non te- me i- ra di ghiac-ci'o di pru- i- ne?⟩

**Seconda parte**

S'ar- mar- ta il cor di mat- tu- ti- no ge- lo,

S'ar- ma ta il cor di mat- tu- ti- no ge- lo, ⟨s'ar-

S'ar- ma ta il cor di mat- tu- ti- no ge- lo, ⟨s'ar-

S'ar- ma ta il cor di mat- tu- ti- no ge- lo,

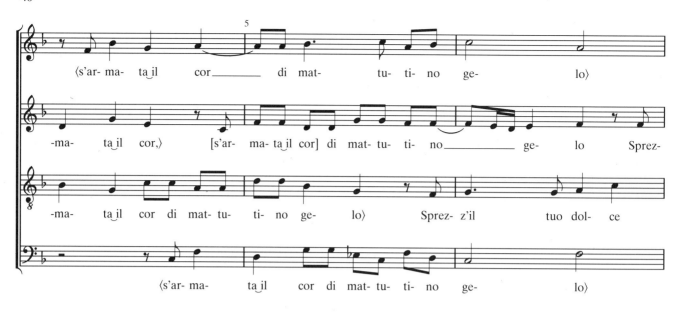

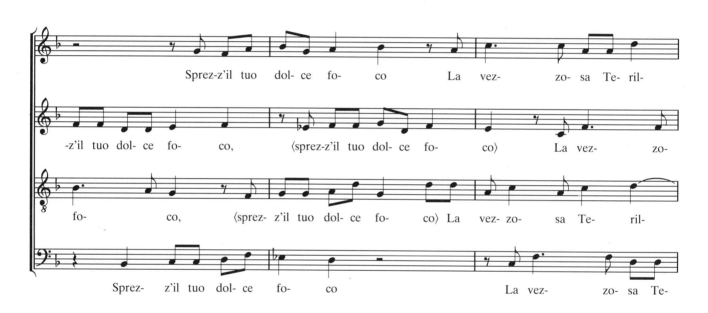

-lo, e dal suo ste- lo Tron- cò la

-lo, ⟨e dal suo ste - lo⟩ Tron- cò la spe- me,

-lo, ⟨e dal suo ste- lo⟩ Tron- cò la spe- me, ⟨tron-

-lo, e dal suo ste- lo⟩ Tron-

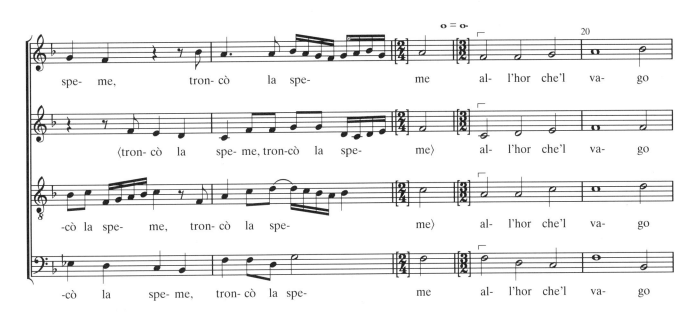

spe- me, tron- cò la spe- me al- l'hor che'l va- go

⟨tron- cò la spe- me, tron- cò la spe- me⟩ al- l'hor che'l va- go

-cò la spe- me, tron- cò la spe- me⟩ al- l'hor che'l va- go

-cò la spe- me, tron- cò la spe- me al- l'hor che'l va- go

fio- re A- pria le fo- glie, al- l'hor che'l va- go fio-re a-pria le fo-

fio- re A- pria le fo- glie, ⟨al- l'hor che'l va- go fio-re a- pria le fo-

fio- re A- pria le fo- glie, ⟨al- l'hor che'l va- go fio-re a- pria le___ fo-

fio- re A- pria le fo- glie, al- l'hor che'l va- go

42

-glie e si mo-stra-va fuo- re, ⟨e si mo-stra-va fuo- re.⟩

-glie⟩ e si mo-stra-va fuo- re, ⟨e si mo-stra-va_____ fuo- re.⟩

-glie⟩ e si mo-stra-va fuo- re, ⟨e si mo-stra-va fuo- re.⟩

fio- re a-pria le fo- glie e si mo-stra- va fuo- re.

**Terza parte**

Scal- da col tuo va- lo- re a po- co a po-

Scal- da col tuo va- lo- re a po- co a po-

Scal- da col tuo va- lo- re a po- co a po-

Scal- da col tuo va- lo- re a po- co a po-

-co, ⟨scal- da col tuo va- lo- re a po- co a po- co⟩ I suoi pen- sier ge-

-co, ⟨scal- da col tuo_ va- lo- re a po- co a po- co⟩ I

-co, ⟨scal- da col tuo va- lo- re a po- co a po- co⟩ I suoi pen-

-co, ⟨scal- da col tuo va- lo- re a po- co a po- co⟩

-la- ti, ⟨i suoi pen- sier ge- la- ti;⟩ Sce- ma l'or- go- glio sì,

suoi pen- sier ge- la- ti, ⟨i suoi pen- sier ge- la- ti;⟩ Sce- ma l'or- go- glio

-sier ge- la- ti, ⟨i suoi pen- sier ge- la- ti;⟩ Sce- ma l'or- go- glio

I suoi pen- sier ge- la- ti, ⟨i suoi pen- sier ge- la- ti;⟩ Sce- ma l'or- go- glio

⟨sce- ma l'or- go- glio sì⟩ che tro- vi lo- co, che tro- vi lo- co,

sì, ⟨sce- ma l'or- go- glio sì⟩ che tro- vi lo- co, che tro- vi lo- co,

sì, ⟨sce- ma l'or- go- glio sì⟩ che tro- vi lo- co, che tro- vi lo- co,

sì, ⟨sce- ma l'or- go- glio sì⟩ che tro- vi lo- co, che tro- vi lo- co,

Do- ve s'ap- pog- gi ne la fred- da men- te, s'ap- pog- gi ne la fred- da

Do- ve s'ap- pog- gi ne la fred- da men- te, s'ap- pog- gi ne la fred- da

Do- ve s'ap- pog- gi ne la fred- da men- te, s'ap- pog- gi ne la fred- da

Do- ve s'ap- pog- gi ne la fred- da men- te, s'ap- pog- gi ni la fred- da

44

men- te     Il mio de- sir via più d'o- gn'al- tro ar- den- te,

men- te     Il mio de- sir via più,    ⟨il mio de- sir via più⟩ d'o-

men- te     Il mio de- sir via più    d'o- gn'al- tro ar- den-

men- te       Il mio de- sir via più    d'o-

⟨il mio de- sir via più d'o- gn'al- tro ar- den- te.⟩

-gn'al- tro ar- den- te,   il mio de- sir via più d'o- gn'al- tro ar- den- te.

- te,   ⟨il mio de- sir via più d'o- gn'al- tro ar- den- te.⟩

-gn'al- tro ar- den- te,   il mio de- sir via più d'o- gn'al- tro ar- den- te.

**Quarta parte**

Non con- sen- tir co- me ne- gl'an- ni an- da- ti,   ⟨non con- sen- tir

Non con- sen- tir co- me ne- gl'an- ni an- da- ti,   ⟨non con- sen-

Non con- sen- tir   co- me ne- gl'an- ni an- da- ti,

Non con- sen- tir   co- me ne- gl'an- ni an- da- ti,

co- me ne-gl'an-ni_an-da- ti⟩ Ch'io fac- ci'_ar- den-t'e mol- li,

-tir co- me ne-gl'an-ni_an-da- ti⟩ Ch'io fac-ci'_ar-den-t'e mol- li,

⟨non con-sen- tir co- me ne- gl'an-ni_an-da- ti,⟩ ne- gl'an-ni_an- da- ti Ch'io fac-ci'_ar-

non con- sen- tir co- me ne- gl'an-ni_an-da- ti Ch'io fac-ci'_ar-den- t'e

⟨ch'io fac- ci'_ar-den- t'e mol- li⟩ Que-st'a- ria di so- spir,

⟨ch'io fac- ci'_ar-den-t'e mol- li⟩ Que-st'a- ria di so- spir, ⟨que-st'a- ria

-den- t'e mol- li, ⟨ch'io fac-ci'_ar- den- t'e mol- li⟩ Que- st'a-ria di so- spir,

mol- li, ⟨ch'io fac-ci'_ar-den- t'e mol- li⟩ Que-st'a- ria di

⟨que-st'a- ria di so- spir,⟩ so- spir, di pian- to_i pra- ti, di pian-

di so- spir,⟩ que-st'a- ria di so- spir, di pian- to_i pra- ti, di pian-

⟨que- st'a- ria di so- spir,⟩ so- spir, di pian- to_i pra- ti, di pian-

so- spir, que-st'a- ria di so- spir, di pian- to_i pra- ti, di pian-

**Quinta parte**

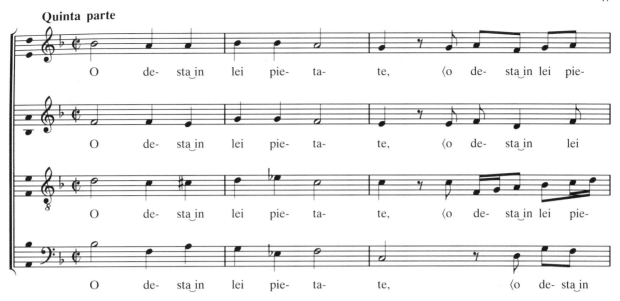

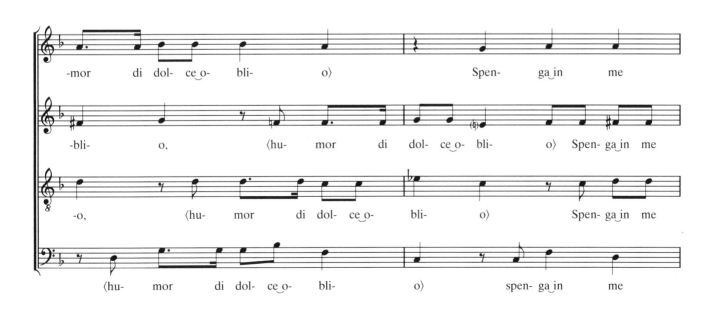

48

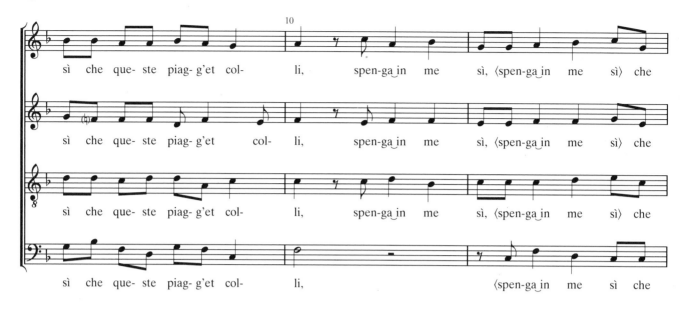

di me- sti pen- sier sia sgom-bro il pet- to.⟩

-to, ⟨et____ di me- sti pen-sier sia sgom-bro il pet- - to.⟩

⟨et di me- sti pen- sier sia sgom-bro il pet- to.⟩

-to, ⟨et di me- sti pen- sier sia sgom-bro il pet- to.⟩

**Sesta parte**

Chi- na le san- t'o- rec- - chie al can- to mi-

Chi- na le san- t'o- rec- chie al can- to

Chi- na le san- t'o-

Chi- na le

-o, ⟨chi- na le san- t'o- rec- chie al can- to

mi- o, ⟨chi- na le san- t'o- rec-chie al can- to mi- o,⟩ Nè

-rec- chie al can- - to mi- o, Nè

san- t'o- rec- chie al can- to mi- o,

-ro- ne, di va- gh'et lie- ti fior, ⟨di va- gh'et lie- te fior⟩ mil- le co-

-ro- ne, di va- gh'et lie- ti fior, ⟨di va- gh'et lie- ti fior⟩ mil- le co-

-ro- ne, di va- gh'et lie- ti fior, ⟨di va- gh'et lie- ti fior⟩ mil- le co-

-ro- ne, ⟨di va- gh'et lie- ti fior mil- le co-

-ro- ne, ⟨di va- gh'et lie- ti fior mil- le co- ro- ne.⟩

-ro- ne, ⟨di va- gh'et lie- ti fior mil- le co- ro- ne.⟩

-ro- ne, ⟨di va- gh'et lie- ti fior mil- le co- ro- ne.⟩

-ro- ne,⟩ di va- gh'et lie- ti fior mil- le co- ro- ne.

# [9] I capegli d'or fin

Madrigali a 4 (1564)

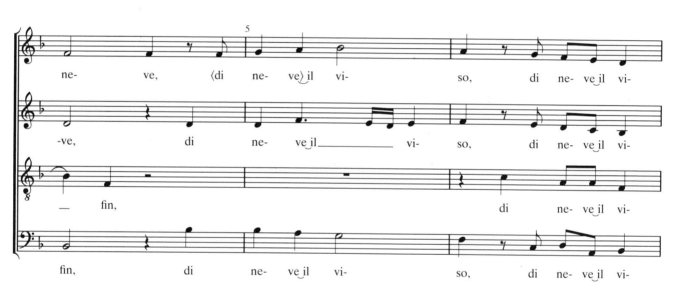

-mi sciol-t'in pa- ra- di- so, ⟨quei va- ghi lu- mi sciol-t'in pa-ra-

-mi sciol- t'in pa- ra- di- so, ⟨quei va- ghi lu- mi sciol- t'in pa-ra-

-mi sciol- t'in pa- ra- di- so, ⟨quei_ va-ghi lu- mi sciol- t'in pa-ra-

Quei va- ghi lu- mi sciol-t'in pa- ra-

-di- so⟩ Per dar al sol, ⟨per dar al sol⟩ qua giù soc- cor- so gra- to, L'an-

-di- so⟩ Per dar al sol, ⟨per dar al sol⟩ qua giù soc- cor- so gra- to, L'an-

-di- so⟩ Per dar al sol, ⟨per dar al sol⟩ qua giù soc- cor- so gra- to, L'an-

-di- so Per dar al sol qua giù soc- cor- so gra- to, L'an-

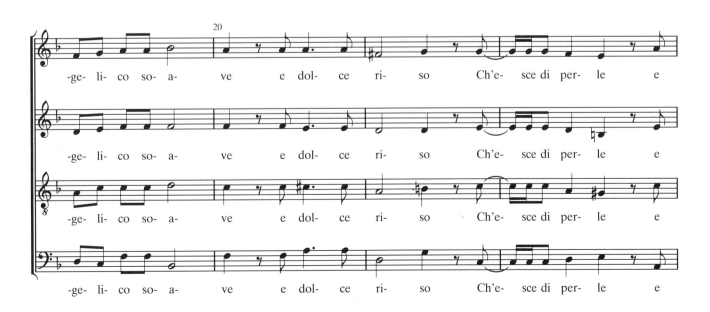

-ge- li- co so- a- ve e dol- ce ri- so Ch'e- sce di per- le e

-ge- li- co so- a- ve e dol- ce ri- so Ch'e- sce di per- le e

-ge- li- co so- a- ve e dol- ce ri- so Ch'e- sce di per- le e

-ge- li- co so- a- ve e dol- ce ri- so Ch'e- sce di per- le e

di co-ral-li or-na- to, Fan u- na Mar- ga- ri- ta sì pre- tio- sa, ⟨fan

di co-ral-li or-na- to, Fan u- na Mar- ga- ri- ta sì pre- tio- sa, ⟨fan

di co-ral-li or-na- to, Fan u- na Mar- ga- ri- ta sì pre- tio- sa, ⟨fan

di co-ral-li or-na- to, Fan

u- na Mar-ga- ri- ta sì pre-tio- sa⟩ Ch'o-gni gem- ma, ⟨ch'o- gni gem-ma⟩ al suo

u- na Mar-ga- ri- ta sì pre-tio- sa⟩ Ch'o-gni gem- ma, ⟨ch'o- gni gem-ma⟩ al suo

u- na Mar-ga- ri- ta sì pre-tio- sa⟩ Ch'o-gni gem- ma, ⟨ch'o- gni gem-ma⟩ al suo

u- na Mar-ga- ri- ta sì pre-tio- sa Ch'o-gni gem- ma, ⟨ch'o- gni gem-ma⟩ al suo

par ve- nir non o- sa.

par ve- nir non o- sa, ⟨ch'o- gni gem-ma al suo par ve-nir non o- sa.⟩

par ve- nir non o- sa, ⟨ch'o- gni gem-ma al suo par ve-nir non o- sa.⟩

par ve- nir non o- sa, ⟨al suo par ve-nir non o- sa.⟩

# [10] Li vostr' occhi

*Madrigali a 4 (1564)*

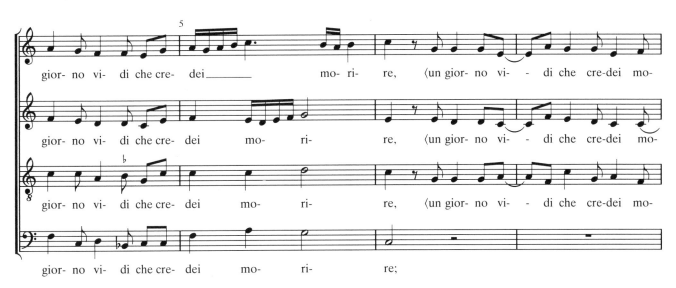

- de te il cor e fa- te- mi gio- i- re, ⟨ren- de- te il cor e
- de te il cor e fa- te- mi gio- i- re, ⟨ren- de- te il cor e
- de te il cor e fa- te- mi gio- i- re, ⟨ren- de- te il cor e
- de te il cor e fa- te- mi gio- i- re

fa- te- mi gio- i- re⟩ E non mi fa- te star più, o vi- so bel- lo, Tan-
fa- te- mi gio- i- re⟩ E non mi fa- te star più, o vi- so bel- lo, Tan-
fa- te- mi gio- i- re⟩ E non mi fa- te star più, o vi- so bel- lo, Tan-
E non mi fa- te star più, o vi- so bel- lo, Tan-

- t'a- di ra- to, ⟨tan- t'a- di- ra- to⟩ che non pos- sa u- dir', u- di-
- t'a- di ra- to, ⟨tan- t'a- di- ra- to⟩ che non pos- sa u- dir', u- di-
- t'a- di ra- to, ⟨tan- t'a- di- ra- to⟩ che non pos- sa u- dir', u- di-
- t'a- di ra- to, ⟨tan- t'a- di- ra- to⟩ che non pos- sa u- dir', u- di-

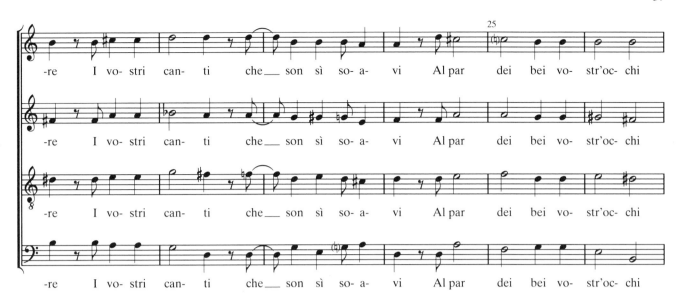

-re I vo- stri can- ti che\_\_ son sì so- a- vi Al par dei bei vo- str'oc- chi

co- sì gra- vi, ⟨al par dei bei\_\_ vo- str'oc- chi co- sì gra- vi.⟩

# [11] Anchor che col partire

Alfonso d'Avalos

*Madrigali a 4 (1564)*

An- chor che col par- ti- re, ⟨an- chor che col __

__ par- ti- re⟩ Io mi sen- to mo- ri- re, ⟨io mi sen- to mo- ri- re,⟩ Par-

-tir vor- rei o- gn'hor, o- gni mo- men- to, Tan-t'[è] il pia- cer ch'io __

sen- to, ⟨tan-t'[è] il pia- cer ch'io sen- to⟩ De la vi- ta ch'a-qui-sto nel ri-tor-

sen- to, ⟨tan-t'[è] il pia- cer ch'io sen- to⟩ De la vi- ta ch'a-qui-sto nel ri- tor-

sen- to, ⟨tan-t'[è] il pia-cer ch'io sen- to⟩ De la vi- ta ch'a-qui-sto nel ri-tor-

sen- to, ⟨tan-t'[è] il pia- cer ch'io sen- to⟩ De la vi- ta ch'a-qui-sto nel ri-tor-

-no. E co- sì mil- l'e mil- le vol- t'il gior- no, ⟨e co- sì mil- l'e mil- le

-no. E co- sì mil- l'e mil- le vol- t'il gior- no, ⟨e co- sì mil- l'e mil- le

-no. E co- sì mil- l'e mil- le vol- t'il gior- no, ⟨e co- sì mil- l'e mil- le

-no. E co- sì mil- l'e mil- le vol- t'il gior- no, ⟨e co- sì mil- l'e mil- le

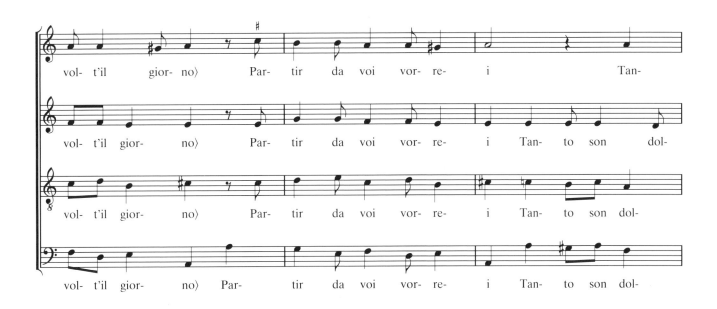

vol- t'il gior- no⟩ Par- tir da voi vor- re- i Tan-

vol- t'il gior- no⟩ Par- tir da voi vor- re- i Tan- to son dol-

vol- t'il gior- no⟩ Par- tir da voi vor- re- i Tan- to son dol-

vol- t'il gior- no⟩ Par- tir da voi vor- re- i Tan- to son dol-

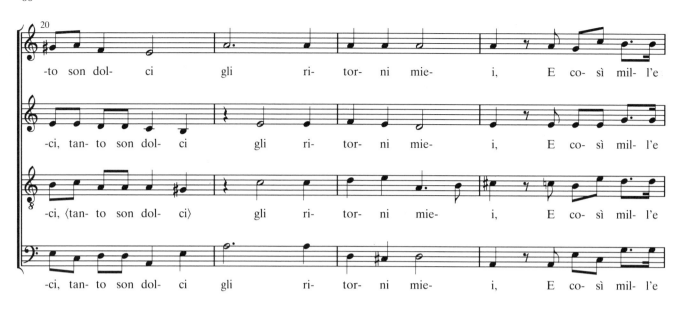

-to son dol- ci gli ri- tor- ni mie- i, E co- sì mil- l'e
-ci, tan- to son dol- ci gli ri- tor- ni mie- i, E co- sì mil- l'e
-ci, ⟨tan- to son dol- ci⟩ gli ri- tor- ni mie- i, E co- sì mil- l'e
-ci, tan- to son dol- ci gli ri- tor- ni mie- i, E co- sì mil- l'e

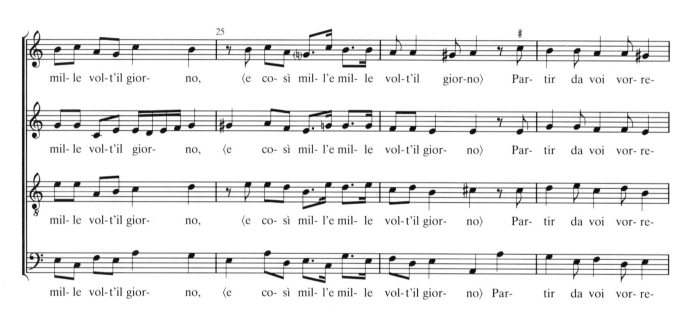

mil- le vol- t'il gior- no, ⟨e co- sì mil- l'e mil- le vol- t'il gior-no⟩ Par- tir da voi vor- re-
mil- le vol- t'il gior- no, ⟨e co- sì mil- l'e mil- le vol- t'il gior- no⟩ Par- tir da voi vor- re-
mil- le vol- t'il gior- no, ⟨e co- sì mil- l'e mil- le vol- t'il gior- no⟩ Par- tir da voi vor- re-
mil- le vol- t'il gior- no, ⟨e co- sì mil- l'e mil- le vol- t'il gior- no⟩ Par- tir da voi vor- re-

-i Tan- to son dol- ci gli ri- tor- ni mie- i.
-i Tan- to son dol- ci, tan- to son dol- ci gli ri- tor- ni mie- i.
-i Tan- to son dol- ci, ⟨tan- to son dol- ci⟩ gli ri- tor- ni mie- i.
-i Tan- to son dol- ci, tan- to son dol- ci gli ri- tor- ni mie- i.

# [12] E se tu, riva, udisti

Jacopo Sannazaro

*Madrigali a 4 (1564)*

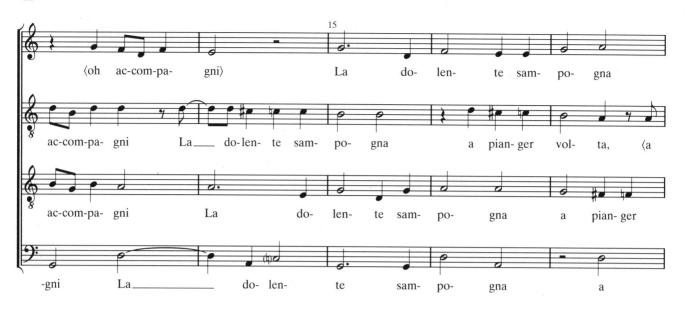

-do, et hor per a- spra sor- te, ⟨et hor per a- spra___ sor- te⟩ Gia-

-do, et hor per a- spra sor- te, ⟨et hor per a- spra___ sor- te⟩ Gia-

-do, et hor per a- spra sor- te, ⟨et hor per a- spra sor- te⟩ Gia-

-do, et hor per a- spra sor- te, ⟨et hor per a- spra sor- te⟩ Gia-

-ce- te per li fiu- mi e per li sta- gni, e per li sta- gni.

-ce- te per li fiu- mi e per li sta- gni, e per li sta - gni.

-ce- te per li fiu- mi e per li sta- gni, e per li___ sta- gni.

-ce- te per li fiu- mi e per li sta- gni, e per li sta- gni.

# [13] Andate, o miei sospiri

*Madrigali a 4 (1564)*

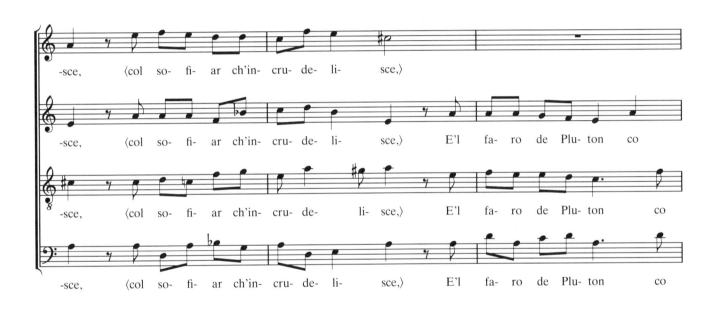

⟨ai- mè, Ca- ron⟩ già sen- to che lan- gui- sce D'ha- ver-m'in grem- bo, ⟨d'ha-

⟨ai- mè, Ca- ron⟩ già sen- to che lan- gui- sce D'ha- ver-m'in grem- bo, ⟨d'ha-

⟨ai- mè, Ca- ron⟩ già sen- to che lan- gui- sce D'ha- ver-m'in grem- bo, ⟨d'ha-

⟨ai- mè, Ca- ron⟩ già sen- to che lan- gui- sce D'ha- ver-m'in grem- bo, ⟨d'ha-

-ver-m'in grem-bo⟩ nei Sti- gi lu- gu- bri, Ma cre- do c'ha-ve- rò tan- ta

-ver-m'in grem-bo⟩ nei Sti- gi lu- gu- bri, Ma cre- do c'ha- ve- rò

-ver-m'in grem-bo⟩ nei Sti- gi lu- gu- bri, Ma cre- do c'ha- ve- rò

-ver-m'in grem-bo⟩ nei Sti- gi lu- gu- bri, Ma cre- do c'ha-ve- rò tan-

a- qua ai lu- mi, Mal- gra- do d'A- tro- pòs, che fa- rò i fiu- mi.

tan- ta a-qua ai lu- mi, Mal- gra- do d'A- tro- pòs, che fa- rò i fiu- mi.

tan- ta a-qua ai lu- mi, Mal- gra- do d'A- tro- pòs, che fa- rò i fiu- mi.

-ta a-qua ai lu- mi, Mal- gra- do d'A- tro- pòs, che fa- rò i fiu- mi.

# [14] Gratia, voi sete

*Madrigali a 4 (1564)*

-ta- de al- tie- ra e ra- ra Chia- ra- men- te si ve- de a ton- d'a
-ta- de al- tie- ra e ra- ra Chia- ra- men- te si ve- de a ton- d'a
-ta- de al- tie- ra e ra- ra Chia- ra- men- te si ve- de a ton- d'a
-ta- de al- tie- ra e ra- ra Chia- ra- men- te si ve- de a ton- d'a

ton- do Ch'ap- pò voi so- la o-gn'al-tra bel- la è al fon- do, Gra- tia d'o-
ton- do Ch'ap- pò voi so- la o-gn'al-tra bel- la è al fon- do, Gra- tia d'o-
ton- do Ch'ap- pò voi so- la o-gn'al-tra bel- la è al____ fon- do, Gra- tia d'o-
ton- do Ch'ap- pò voi so- la o-gn'al-tra bel- la è al fon- do, Gra- tia d'o-

-gni vir- tu- de al mon-do chia- ra, al,____ al mon-do chia- ra.
-gni vir- tu- de al mon-do chia- ra, al,____ al mon-do chia- ra.
-gni vir- tu- de al mon-do chia- ra, al,____ al mon-do chia- ra.
-gni vir- tu- de al mon-do chia- ra, al,____ al mon-do chia- ra.

# [15] Piangi, colle sacrato

Jacopo Sannazaro

*Madrigali a 4 (1564)*

[Prima parte]

Canto

Alto

Tenore

Basso

Pian- gi, col-

Pian- gi, col- le sa-

Pian- gi, col- le_____ sa- cra-

Pian- gi, col- le sa- cra- - to o-

-le sa- cra- t'o- pa- - co e fo- sco, Et voi ca- ve____ spe- lon- ch'e

-cra- t'o- pa- co e fo- sco, Et voi ca- ve____ spe- lon- ch'e

-t'o- pa- co e fo- sco, Et voi ca- ve____ spe- lon- ch'e

-pa- co e fo- sco, Et voi ca- ve____ spe- lon- ch'e

grot- te o- scu- re, U- lu- lan- do ve- ni- te a pian- ger no- sco, u-

grot- te o- scu- re, U- lu- lan- do ve- ni- te a pian- ger no- sco, u-

grot- te o- scu- re, U- lu- lan- do ve- ni- te a pian- ger no- sco, u-

grot- te o- scu- re, U- lu- lan- do ve- ni- te a pian- ger no- sco.

- lu- lan- do, ⟨u- - lu- lan- do⟩ ve- ni- te a pian- ger no-

- lu- lan- do, ⟨u- - lu- lan- do⟩ ve- ni- te a pian- ger_____ no-

- lu- lan- do, ⟨u- - lu- lan- do⟩ ve- ni- te a pian- ger no-

Pian-

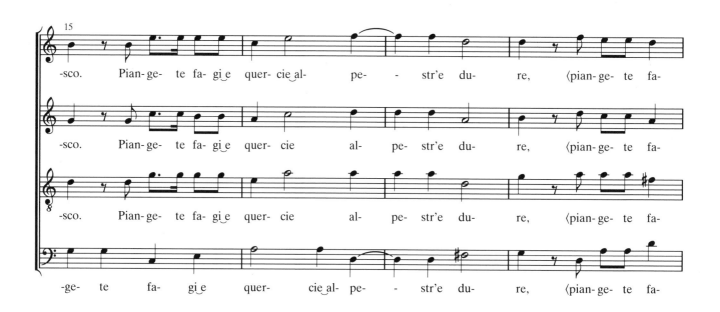

-sco. Pian- ge- te fa- gi e quer- cie al- pe- - str'e du- re, ⟨pian- ge- te fa-

-sco. Pian- ge- te fa- gi e quer- cie al- pe- str'e du- re, ⟨pian- ge- te fa-

-sco. Pian- ge- te fa- gi e quer- cie al- pe- str'e du- re, ⟨pian- ge- te fa-

-ge- te fa- gi e quer- cie al- pe- - str'e du- re, ⟨pian- ge- te fa-

-gi e quer-cie al-pe- str'e du- re,⟩ E_____ pian-gen- do, pian- gen- do, nar- ra-

-gi e quer-cie al-pe- str'e du- re,⟩ E_____ pian-gen- do, pian-gen- do, nar-

-gi e quer-cie al-pe- str'e du- re,⟩ E_____ pian-gen- do, pian- gen- do, nar- ra-

-gi e quer-cie al-pe- str'e du- re,⟩ E_____ pian-gen- do, pian-gen- do, nar-

**Seconda parte**

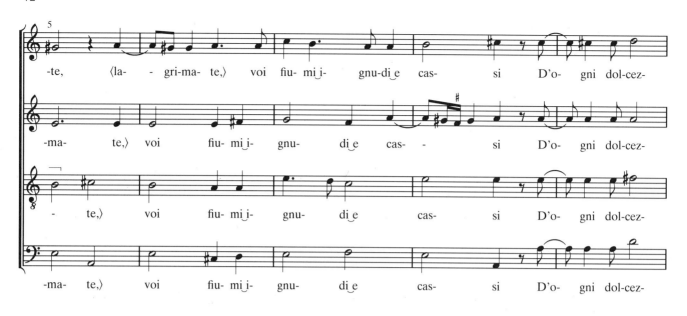

-te, ⟨la- -gri-ma- te,⟩ voi fiu- mi i- gnu-di e cas- si D'o- gni dol-cez-

-ma- te,⟩ voi fiu- mi i- gnu- di e cas - si D'o- gni dol-cez-

- te,⟩ voi fiu- mi i- gnu- di e cas- si D'o- gni dol-cez-

-ma- te,⟩ voi fiu- mi i- gnu- di e cas- si D'o- gni dol-cez-

-za, ⟨d'o- gni dol- cez- za,⟩ e voi, fon-ta- ne e ri- vi, Fer- ma- te il cor-

-za, ⟨d'o- gni dol- cez- za,⟩ e voi, fon-ta- ne e ri- vi, Fer- ma- te il cor-

-za, ⟨d'o- gni dol- cez- za,⟩ e voi, fon-ta- ne e ri- vi, Fer- ma- te il_____ cor-

-za, ⟨d'o- gni dol- cez- za,⟩ e voi, fon-ta- ne e ri- vi, Fer- ma- te il cor-

-so, e re- te- ne- te i pas- si. E tu, ⟨e tu,⟩ e tu che

-so, e re- te- ne- te i pas- si. E tu, e tu che fra le sel-

-so, e re- te- ne- te i pas- si. E tu, ⟨e tu,⟩ e tu che fra le

-so, e re- te- ne- te i pas- si. E tu, e tu, e tu che fra le

fra le sel-ve oc-cul- ta vi- vi, ⟨e tu che fra le sel- ve oc-cul- ta vi- vi,⟩ E- cho me-

-ve oc- cul- ta vi- vi, ⟨e tu che fra le sel- ve oc-cul- ta vi- vi,⟩ E- cho me-

sel- ve oc- cul- ta vi- vi, ⟨e tu che fra le sel- ve oc-cul- ta vi- vi,⟩ E- cho me-

sel- ve oc- cul- ta vi- vi, ⟨e tu che fra le sel- ve oc-cul- ta vi- vi,⟩ E- cho me-

-sta, ri- spon- di, ri- spon- di a le pa- ro- le E quan-t'io

-sta, ri- spon- di, ri- spon- di a le pa- ro- le E quan-t'io

-sta, ri- spon- di, ri- spon- di a le pa- ro- le E quan-t'io

-sta, ri- spon- di, ri- spon- di a le pa- ro- le E quan-t'io

par- lo per li____ tron-chi scri- vi, ⟨e quan-t'io par-lo per li tron-chi scri- vi.⟩

par- lo per li____ tron-chi scri- vi, ⟨e quan-t'io par-lo per li tron- chi____scri- vi.⟩

par- lo per li tron- chi____scri- vi, ⟨e quan-t'io par- lo per li tron-chi scri- vi.⟩

par- lo per li tron- chi scri- vi, ⟨e quan-t'io par-lo per li tron-chi scri- vi.⟩

# [16] Piangete, valli

Jacopo Sannazaro

*Madrigali a 4 (1564)*

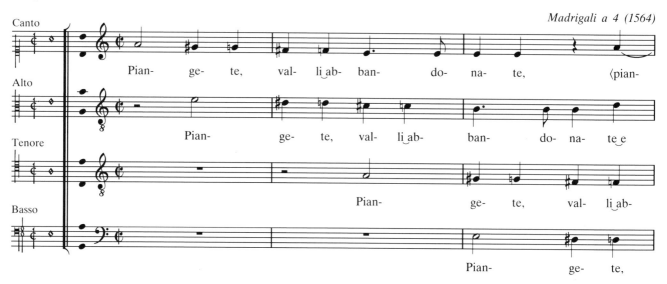

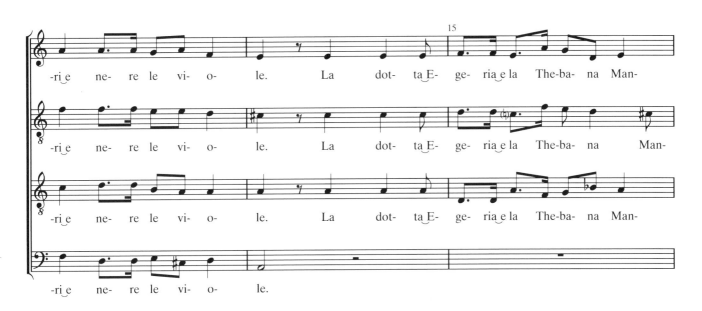

⟨con su- bi- to fu- ror,⟩ con su- bi- to fu- ror mor- te

-ror, ⟨con su- bi- to fu- ror,⟩ con su- bi- to fu- ror mor- te_____

-to fu- ror, ⟨con su- bi- to fu- ror,⟩ con su- bi- to fu- ror mor-

Con su- bi- to fu- ror, ⟨con su- bi- to fu- ror,⟩ con su- bi- to fu- ror mor-

n'ha tol- ta, mor- te n'ha tol- ta. Ri- co- min-cia- te, o

___ n'ha tol- ta, ⟨mor- te n'ha tol- ta.⟩ Ri- co- min-cia- te, o Mu-

- te n'ha tol- ta, ⟨mor- te n'ha tol- ta.⟩ Ri- co- min-cia- te, o

- te n'ha tol- ta, mor- te n'ha tol- ta. Ri- co- min-cia-

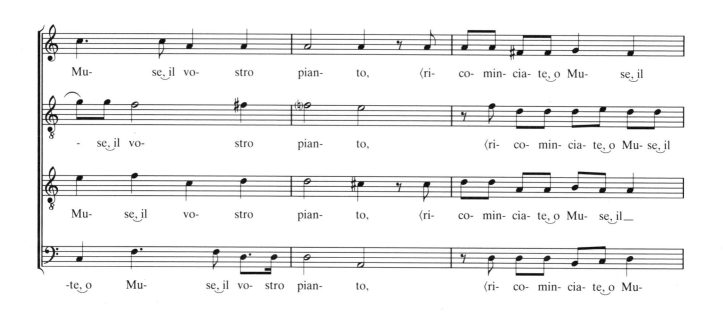

Mu- se, il vo- stro pian- to, ⟨ri- co- min- cia- te, o Mu- se, il

- se, il vo- stro pian- to, ⟨ri- co- min- cia- te, o Mu- se, il

Mu- se, il vo- stro pian- to, ⟨ri- co- min- cia- te, o Mu- se, il___

-te, o Mu- se, il vo- stro pian- to, ⟨ri- co- min- cia- te, o Mu-

vo- stro_____ pian- to,) il vo- stro pian - to.

vo- stro pian- to,) il vo- stro pian- to.

vo- stro pian- to,) il vo- stro pian- to.

-se il vo- stro pian- to,) il vo- stro pian- to.

# [17] Ardir, senno, virtù

*Madrigali a 4 (1564)*

Canto

Alto

Tenore

Basso

Ar- dir, ar- dir, sen- no, vir- tù, bel- lez- za e fe- de, La

fa- m'in ter- ra co- m'im- mor- tal De- a, Qual Di- o non mos-

-se pre- st'il san- to pie- de Quan- do co- nob- be del ver- mo l'I- de-

-a, ⟨quan- do co- nob- be del ver- mo l'I- de- a?⟩ Giu- non in lei

-a, ⟨quan- do co- nob- be del ver- mo l'I- de- a?⟩ Giu- non in lei

-a, ⟨quan- do co- nob- be del ver- mo l'I- de- a?⟩ Giu- non in lei

-a? Giu- non in lei

con la ric- chez- za sie- de Mi - ner- va sag- gia, ⟨Mi-

con la ric- chez- za sie- de Mi - ner- va sag- gia, ⟨Mi-

con la ric- chez- za sie- de Mi - ner- va sag- gia, ⟨Mi-

con la ric- chez- za sie- de Mi - ner- va sag- gia, ⟨Mi-

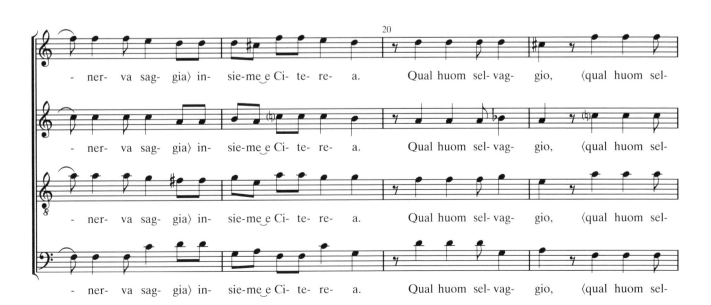

- ner- va sag- gia⟩ in- sie-me e Ci- te- re- a. Qual huom sel- vag- gio, ⟨qual huom sel-

- ner- va sag- gia⟩ in- sie-me e Ci- te- re- a. Qual huom sel- vag- gio, ⟨qual huom sel-

- ner- va sag- gia⟩ in- sie-me e Ci- te- re- a. Qual huom sel- vag- gio, ⟨qual huom sel-

- ner- va sag- gia⟩ in- sie-me e Ci- te- re- a. Qual huom sel- vag- gio, ⟨qual huom sel-

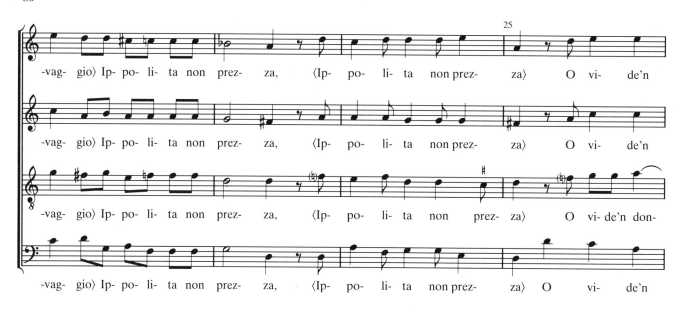

-vag- gio⟩ Ip- po- li- ta non prez- za, ⟨Ip- po- li- ta non prez- za⟩ O vi- de'n

-vag- gio⟩ Ip- po- li- ta non prez- za, ⟨Ip- po- li- ta non prez- za⟩ O vi- de'n

-vag- gio⟩ Ip- po- li- ta non prez- za, ⟨Ip- po- li- ta non prez- za⟩ O vi- de'n don-

-vag- gio⟩ Ip- po- li- ta non prez- za, ⟨Ip- po- li- ta non prez- za⟩ O vi- de'n

don- na mai più gran va- ghez- za, più gran va- ghez- za?

don- na mai più gran va- ghez- za, più gran va- ghez- za?

- na mai più gran va- ghez- za, più gran va- ghez- za?

don- na mai più gran va- ghez- za, più gran va- ghez- za?

# [18] Dialogo a 8 voci: Donna, l'ardente fiamma

*Madrigali a 4 (1564)*

# Book 4, Madrigali a 5 (1584/85)

# [1] Sculpio ne l'alma Amore

*Madrigali a 5 (1584/85)*

# [2] Come esser può

Madrigali a 5 (1584/85)

94

*Alto should sing an eighth note here. See Preface, p. xiv, for discussion.

\*See m. 39.

# [3] Va lieto a mort' il core

*Madrigali a 5 (1584/85)*

# [4] Vedesti, Amor, giamai

*Madrigali a 5 (1584/85)*

# [5] Gel' ha madonna il core

Torquato Tasso

*Madrigali a 5 (1584/85)*

# [6] Thirsi morir volea

Battista Guarini

*Madrigali a 5 (1584/85)*

112

Seconda parte

114

-ti Di mor- te sì so- a- ve e sì gra- di- ta Che per
-ti Di mor- te sì so- a- ve e sì gra- di- ta Che per an- co mo-rir,
Di mor- te sì so- a- ve e sì gra- di- ta Che per an- co mo-rir, ⟨che per
-ti e sì_____ gra- di- ta Che per
Di mor- te sì so- a- ve e sì gra- di- ta Che per an- co mo-rir,

an- co mo- rir tor- na- r'in vi- ta,
che per an- co mo-rir tor- na- r'in vi- ta, che per an- co mo-
an- co mo- rir,⟩ che per an- co mo- rir tor- na- r'in vi- ta, che per an- co mo-
an- co mo- rir, che per an- co mo-
⟨che per an- co mo- rir⟩ tor- na- r'in vi- ta,

che per an- co mo-rir tor-na- r'in vi- ta, tor- na- r'in vi- ta.
-rir tor- na- r'in vi- ta, ⟨tor- na- r'in vi- ta.⟩
-rir, ⟨che per an- co mo-rir⟩ tor- na- r'in vi- ta, ⟨tor- na- r'in_____ vi- ta.⟩
-rir tor- na- r'in vi- ta.
che per an- co mo-rir tor-na- r'in vi- ta, tor- na- r'in vi- ta.

# [7] Io piansi un tempo

*Madrigali a 5 (1584/85)*

118

# [8] Parto da voi

*Madrigali a 5 (1584/85)*

# [9] Mi suggean l'api il mele

Girolamo Casone

*Madrigali a 5 (1584/85)*

# [10] Poi che 'l mio largo pianto

Madrigali a 5 (1584/85)

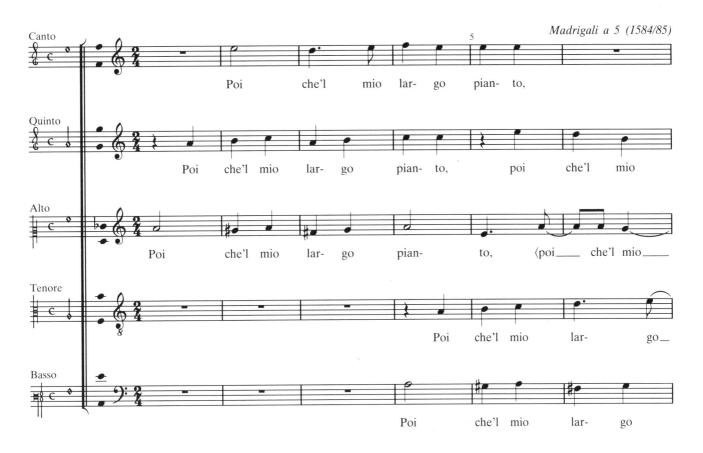

# [11] Poi che ne' bei sospiri

*Madrigali a 5 (1584/85)*

140

# [12] Scoprirò l'ardor mio

*Madrigali a 5 (1584/85)*

Canto: Sco- pri- rò l'ar- dor mio,

Alto: Sco- pri- rò l'ar- dor mio, ⟨sco-

Quinto: Sco- pri- rò l'ar- dor mio

Tenore: Sco- pri-

Basso: Sco- pri- rò

⟨sco- pri- rò l'ar- dor mio⟩ con dir ch'io mo- ro, ⟨con dir—

-pri- rò l'ar- dor mio⟩ con dir ch'io

con dir, con dir ch'io mo- ro, ⟨con

-rò l'ar- dor mio con dir ch'io mo- ro.

l'ar- dor mio con dir ch'io mo- ro, ⟨con dir ch'io mo-

148

# [13] Se voi set' il mio cor

*Madrigali a 5 (1584/85)*

152

# [14] Che fa hoggi il mio sole

*Madrigali a 5 (1584/85)*

# [15] Chi mov' il piè

Gabriel Fiamma

**Prima parte**

*Madrigali a 5 (1584/85)*

162

**Seconda parte**

164

# [16] È ben ragion

*Madrigali a 5 (1584/85)*

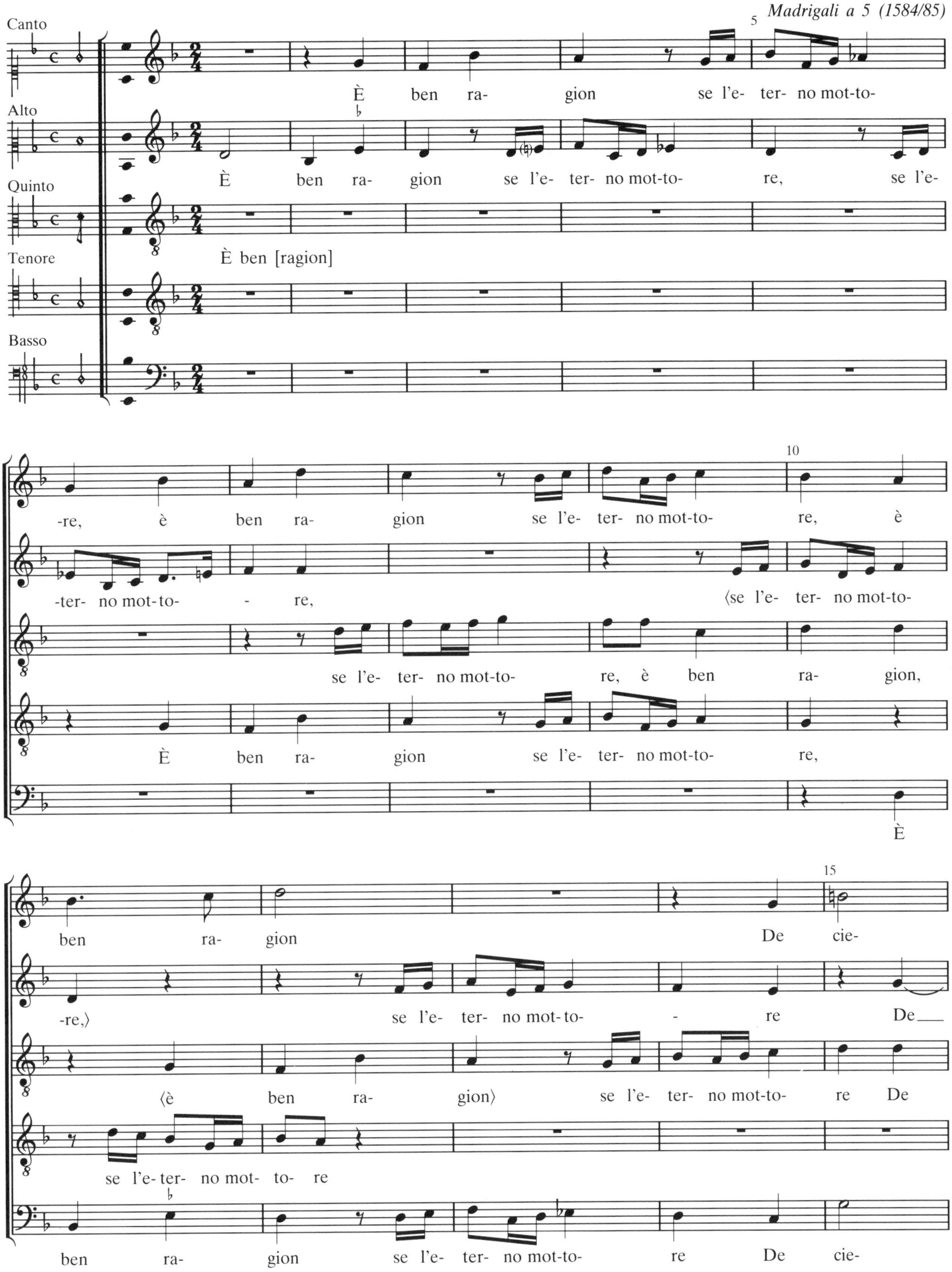

# [17] Canzone: O sola, o senza par

**Prima stanza**

*Madrigali a 5 (1584/85)*

**Seconda stanza**

*From* Fiamma ardente a 5 (1586)

# [1] Mirate che m'ha fatto

*Fiamma ardente a 5 (1586)*

# [2] Date la vela al vento

*Fiamma ardente a 5 (1586)*

# [3] Bene mio, tu m'hai lasciato

*Fiamma ardente a 5 (1586)*

200

# [4] Un' ape esser vorei

*Fiamma ardente a 5 (1586)*

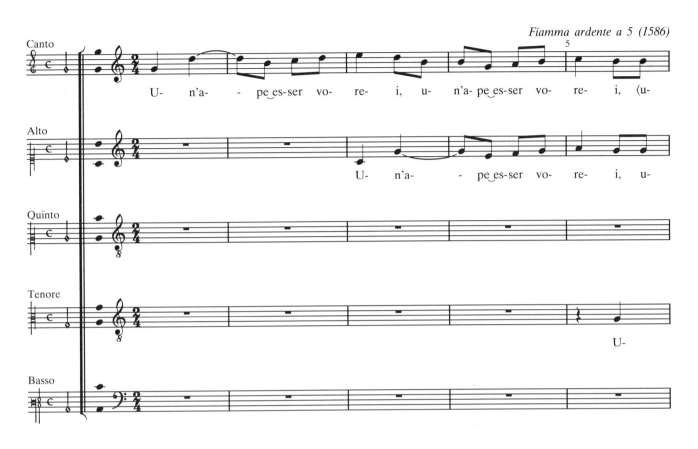

# [5] Gioia mia dolc' e cara

*Fiamma ardente a 5 (1586)*

# [6] Dolci sospir'

*Fiamma ardente a 5 (1586)*

210

# [7] Lo core mio

*Fiamma ardente a 5 (1586)*

# [8] Vola, vola, pensier

Torquato Tasso

*Fiamma ardente a 5 (1586)*

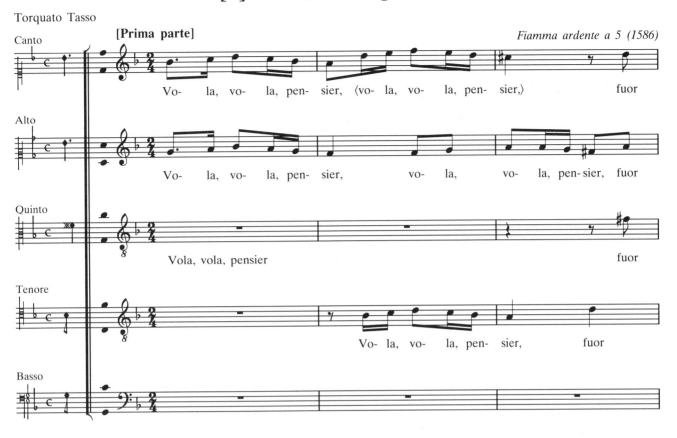

Canto: Vo- la, vo- la, pen- sier, ⟨vo- la, vo- la, pen- sier,⟩ fuor

Alto: Vo- la, vo- la, pen- sier, vo- la, vo- la, pen- sier, fuor

Quinto: Vola, vola, pensier fuor

Tenore: Vo- la, vo- la, pen- sier, fuor

Basso:

del mio pet- to, vo-la, vo- la, pen-sier, fuor del mio pet- to, vo- la, vo- la, pen- sier, ⟨vo-la, vo- la, pen-

del mio pet- to, vo- la, pen-sier, fuor del mio pet- to, vo- la, vo- la, pen- sier, ⟨vo- la,

del mio pet- to, vo-la, vo- la, pen- sier, fuor del mio pet- to,

del mio pet- to, fuor del mio pet- to, vo-la, vo- la, pen-

Vo-la, vo- la, pen- sier, fuor del mio pet- to,

214

216

# [9] Tutte l'offese

*Fiamma ardente a 5 (1586)*

# [10] Canzone: Partomi, donna

224

228

234

# [11] Occhi leggiadri

*Fiamma ardente a 5 (1586)*

# [12] Questa crudel

*Fiamma ardente a 5 (1586)*

# [13] 'Na volta m'hai gabbato

*Fiamma ardente a 5 (1586)*

# [14] Con tue lusinghe, Amore

*Fiamma ardente a 5 (1586)*

246